WAND

Chuck Champlin

ISBN: 978-1-64314-675-1 (Paperback)
        978-1-64314-676-8 (Hardback)
        978-1-64314-677-5 (E-book)

AuthorsPress
California, USA
www.authorspress.com

INTRODUCTION 2021

"WAND" IS A NOVEL of late 1980's Los Angeles when "the Internet" was more than 10 years in the future and a video project called "Hole in Space" dramatically showcased the coming ability to create face-to-face dialogue over distance. That project by artists Kit Galloway and Sherrie Rabinowitz linked street scenes in Los Angeles and New York via video and satellite technology. For two days, people in those cities found themselves speaking to each other, face to face, through a conceptual "hole in space."

Today, the internet and "Zoom" make such contacts commonplace, yet still mind-bending and futuristic.

"Wand" reminds us that pens and television antennas are, in fact, magical in their ongoing potential to improve life on our planet. Distance no longer separates people by wealth or class; we are all people of the earth. Writing, and our global communications, link us in understanding and cooperation.

GOING FOR THE TURNER PRIZE

"Wand" was inspired by the media mogul Ted Turner, founder of CNN. Turner's "Tomorrow Fellowship Award," announced in 1989, offered $500,000 for a novel that visualized solutions to global problems. Some 2,500 novels were submitted for the prize, including this one.

A lead character in this book is a homeless man named John, who joins the narrator in using the video tele-communications concept to showcase new ideas and promote dialogue among communities.

To submit the book for the Turner Prize, I needed a postmark by latest midnight, December 31, 1989. I believed I could get that important date-stamp at the downtown Los Angeles post office called "Terminal Annex." But when I arrived there with my precious package, the building was closed and dark!

Amazingly, a homeless man emerged from the bushes by Terminal Annex and said I could drive to Los Angeles Airport where a post office was open. Feeling doubtful but desperate, I took this homeless man into my car, and we drove across town late on this New Year's Eve. Sure enough, a small office in a parking lot at LAX was open, lit by a single lightbulb, and even 20 minutes after midnight was still stamping envelopes with the Dec. 31 date!

While this worthy book did not win the Turner prize, my ego was satisfied. A year's work was preserved. And here it is, 30 years later, ready I hope, to inspire you!

Chuck Champlin
Yuba City, California
September, 2021

ONE

Hello, Dear Reader. Welcome to the fun house, in the privacy of my own skull. I am the animator, presenting dreams you could see in the movies, if they ever got made.

Open the door, here comes a train, woo Woo!

Paint a black circle on the wall, see the demons jump out!

Like the old Fleischer Superman cartoons, I can fly and move mountains. With the ease of a wish, cities perch on clouds. Freeways leap across the sky and right over the traffic jams. Life is a wonderful place.

Get it? Just like yours, my head is a theater with a screen running non-stop, stories that defy the laws of gravity and behavior. Admission is free. I can sit and watch for hours.

Out here, in my humble apartment, not much to do today. That's normal. Yesterday, not much to do either. That's what I did.

But we can still have some fun. Let's watch cartoons on TV!

My personal favorite is Chuck Jones' "One Froggy Evening." At Warner Bros., they used to call them "one-offs" because they'd only make one like it, not like the Daffy's or Bugs Bunny's. In Froggy, this workman is tearing down a building and finds a box in the foundation. When he opens it, a frog jumps out and starts singing show tunes in a big theatrical voice.

"Hello my baby, hello m'honey, hello my ragtime gal!"

The man knows he's gonna make a fortune, so he rents a hall and sells tickets. When the curtain opens, the frog won't sing! He'll only do it when no one's looking. The guy is wrecked. It really makes my day when that cartoon comes on. Such frustration. Should have put the toad on tape!

Made me think: why not put my brain on tape? Thus, this! Don't worry; by the time you get it, this'll be sanitized. But why not put the opera on record, I thought? Make my very own screamplay? Maybe I'll look back one day and understand it. Seems to me, a personality is a terrible enemy to have. Imagine that frog sitting RIGHT THERE, ready to sing, but he won't do it, not in public. It's a lonely life with nowhere to go but INWARDS and downwards. Like I said, nothing to do today.

But who cares, really? The scene here is just about perfect when I've just made a pitcher of fresh orange juice. I sit back on a warm morning in my apartment with the TV on and the sun shining in. Kitty here is cozy in my lap. Beloved L.A. Times is before me, ready for unwrapping. It's times like this, sitting here, waiting for courage and inspiration, I can really enjoy my disability.

Hey, I should have gotten an Academy Award. "The Day of the Spaghetti Sauce Avalanche," directed by, produced by, starring… me…made on location at The Pizza Place, Pico and Westwood right here in West L.A.

All the noise! Everybody in the place was looking, and worried. Thanks to some very careful planning, an entire shelf of tomato paste cans came down on me, pizza sauce all over. I was screaming when Mr. Katch found me. "Jesus. Chris. Are you alright?!" I felt sorry for the guy. I'll never forget his face.

It wasn't Katch's fault I didn't like it there. Bored. Beneath me, I guess. Should have finished art school. But, hey, situations are fine now. The doctor understood when I said I couldn't walk, couldn't see straight. It's just a little thing, you understand. And there really is a problem that I'm working out here. This is serious stuff. Meanwhile the state's paying. Katch is paying. I'm on recuperation of the sort a lot of people could really use. Time to think. Mainly, the system works!

OK, it's boring sometimes, this life.

I listen to commercials for computer schools, court reporters. Can't see working that hard.

I think my drawings are getting better. My pencil study of a glass of orange juice is showing some real feeling.

If you want to know the truth, I guess what I'm really looking for is something meaningful—maybe in the paper here. Something really great, like Bungee Jumper off the Eiffel Tower maybe.

Better yet, something with some profit sharing, or stock options. Listen, I'm trying to tell you: I'm a very creative guy, just a little restrained sometimes, maybe blocked. Go ahead, just find me a situation that calls for real creative leadership. I know I could make a difference!

For instance, who likes to see the world so messed up? Not me. Right here in the paper it says, homelessness reaches crisis proportions. And the gangs are worse than ever; drive-by shootings are up again over last year. Mayor says, "We've got to give these people something to do."

That's what I say, too. The movie screens kick in with ideas, visions. But what are those gangs anyway? Aren't they like local political parties? All that spray-painted graffiti is corporate logos in the making, or personal coats of arms, seems to me. The kids have just got their agendas screwed up, don't they? Killing each other, over stupid turf wars. Why don't we call them out? Challenge them to do something with their organizations and their desire for self-expression. Hell, anybody wants to make a mark, wants a piece of the landscape. The kids may be dumb, but they're not stupid, right?

Here's the vision: Why not put those kids to work at their own game—drawing some personality for themselves, their community? There's a crying need to say something, be something. Take it, world! Do something with it!

I've got this TV show idea, "Our Gangs," just like the Our Gang comedies. Sure, put some humor in it. Got to deflate the horror a little bit, that's what makes this issue so big. Seems like the show could recognize the gang logos in some way, the personalities, and challenge the kids to do something good in the name of their groups. Maybe "The good-guy gangs." If you needed to, you could withdraw recognition when they're bad.

Like: "Tonight! Our Gangs, brought to you by The Crips and the Bloods of South Central L.A., but not by the Killers of 124th Street who shot a ten-year-old girl last week, oohhh nooooo!"

It's a fun house in here all right. But I keep a straight face about that sort of thing. Imagine the reaction if I suggested that idea to somebody?

Somebody knocks on the door of my little apartment. I'm not used to being interrupted in my morning reveries.

Open the door. It's a tall man in a sport coat with a green tie. A friendly green. Matches my Kermit the Frog watch. He seems nice enough.

"Hello, my name is Robin Seesman and I'm from the Institute of Psychological Difficulty and Clarification. How are you Mr. Walkman? Chris Walkman, is that right?"

"Yes, that's it." His voice is clear and friendly. My back and legs are suddenly shooting with pain. I stoop into a wincing caricature of myself.

"Mr. Walkman, I'm sorry if my visit is causing you additional discomfort. First of all, here is an envelope that was sitting on your doormat."

He hands me an envelope that says, "Mr. Walkman, YOU MAY HAVE ALREADY WON...!" Great. Funny I didn't hear the mailman come by, and it seems early.

Mr. Seesman pleasantly continues, though he's hard to see through the lightning bolts of pain that sear my eyes. I hope he notices.

He says, "The only other thing I wanted to do was introduce myself, offer you my card, and alert you to the fact that we are available to help you, should you ever need our assistance in future."

He delicately hands me a card balanced between his first and second fingers as if it were a feather.

"At the Institute, we are very concerned about the recovery of people who seem to have psychological difficulties added to their physical challenges. I do not mean to insult you, and I pray I am not, Mr. Walkman, but sometimes we have found that special, ah, coaching, can be very effective in assisting people in their recovery and in making extra special use of their lives." He smiles sincerely.

Because of my intensely imagined pain and suffering as well as my desire to have my apartment back to myself, I am DEEPLY insulted, and I endeavor to show this.

Looking at his card from a bent over position I say with a croak, "Mr. Seesman, I have suffered some fairly distressing disturbances in my life in recent months. I hope you will understand when I say, thank you for your concern, but for now I beg to be left alone. I am pursuing therapeutic treatments. Now thank you so much for your time."

The world is not ready for me. I am not ready for the world. I move to close the door.

"Mr. Walkman, of course I understand. I'll be in touch in a short time, to see how you're doing. But please do call me if I can be of assistance, won't you?"

"Of course. Now goodbye." I close the door, then peek through the curtains to watch him walk away from the door. He stops, looks at his watch, looks at the door again, then walks away.

I look at his card. I thought the Institute of Psychological Difficulty and Clarification was a state institution of some sort. No sign of it. I drop the card in the can.

As for the envelope, the fact that I may have already won is always of mild interest. Open, says me. I read.

"Hello, Mr. Walkman.

"Please DO NOT STOP READNG until you fully understand the MAGNITUDE OF THE OPPORTUNITY THAT NOW LIES IN YOUR HANDS.

"Yes, you Mr. Walkman"—I love those personalized printers—"may have won the opportunity to HELP SAVE THE WORLD WITH ALL REASONABLE EXPENSES PAID. All you need to do, and please DO IT RIGHT NOW, before another moment of your precious life goes by—is come visit our office.

"Please be assured that no salesman will call. If you are chosen, you will participate in a short discussion, and then you will be awarded the first installment of the CASH YOU WLL NEED TO MAKE A DIFFERENCE.

"Yes, this is truly a unique moment in the history of the world, because for the first time a formal process has begun of making the world a better place, driven by dedicated, highly motivated people...like you.

"Yes, Mr. Walkman, you have resources you may not even be aware of: to change things, to help us all think of better ways to live. If you believe that, now is the time to act, while this unique opportunity is still before you.

"Come IMMEDIATELY to the beautiful Skyler Building in Downtown Los Angeles and find out if you are one of the lucky ones who will start on a quest...to making a real difference.

"Come visit me personally, Mr. Thomas Hugo, in room 3100, to find out about the first exciting step into what could be the rest of your life.

"Please, do it now!

"Signed, Thomas Hugo, President, Lifetime Adventures." This is a bit strange if you ask me.

I suppose I might be interested in saving the world if I had a little more time available. Imagine trying to save the world? Ridiculous. That's why we've got presidents.

As I think about it, I realize what a lot I have to do today. I think I'm ready to undertake something important, like a still-life drawing of my feet.

What could this stupid thing mean by "save the world?" If you ask me, it's just about unsavable anyway. Everybody's pretty much set in their ways. The poor are gonna be poor. Once you're poor, it's very hard to learn any other skill.

"Reasonable expenses paid?" I wonder how much you'd need to save the world exactly. Say you decided to buy food for everyone. A dollar at meal times—hmm—seven billion people is it now, last time I counted. With the money that General Motors makes, you could almost feed the world for a week. Maybe even at McDonald's.

Wonder who's doing this? Save the world? Obviously, a volunteer operation. Who'd take on such a thing? Wonder if they'd pay flight expenses? Say, that's an idea right there. A skiing trip, with a side trip to save the world.

I think they got me pegged, about the resources I may not be aware of. I have hardly any resources I'm aware of.

But then I imagine that the animator/designer got a big movie deal. All the sketches and character studies he's worked on for years, the big ideas, the arching skyways and floating cities are set for production. What a dream, what a dream.

Should I dare imagine that I could do something? Courage, what a concept!

Hell, I guess I might be up for something different.

Who was that talking, anyway? Who would make a stupid offer like that?

This is crazy. But so am I, that's for sure.

Damn. Maybe...OK, I'll go.

Actually, I think I'll stay here, it's comfy.

Go.

I really admire decisive people.

You know, that cat brought in fleas and now the place is thick with the monsters. I've got to set off one of the bombs first. And what about the newspaper, and the rest of the cartoons?

It's not a pretty sight as I take myself by the collar and THROW MYSELF OUT THE DOOR.

Nose-pressed against the bus window, our ship plows through a sea of daylight haze.

When I look at Los Angeles at night, especially from a plane, the place is exciting. One of my many fleeting girl friends said it's like a pirate's treasure spread on his sheets of black velvet. That girl friend is lying there naked every time I think of that.

The nighttime version of L.A. seems like the center of the world, setting the pace with entertainment and style and ideas. The races come together like nowhere except New York, but you don't have to be a masochist to live here, unless you have something against death by gangs or smog.

Anyway, L.A. is a great concept at night.

The daytime, like now, is something else. The real, sorry thing drives the excitement right away, suffocates it in millions of motley sad people. Daytime, the magic potential of all those people turns into some gigantic responsibility that makes me want to get back in bed. It's why they invented cartoons, I'm sure.

It's crazy to feel responsible for all the people, but I do, don't know why. All that energy going to waste. I sort of admire the Egyptians. Maybe we should build a pyramid, a giant one, right next to the Los Angeles River. Something for all the people to do. I can hear the crack of the whips. Maybe that's what I would do.

The bus roars arrival at the corner of Hope and Fifth. I jump off this bus, plop down on my sneakers, knowing so much more than all the people around. I'm unaccustomed to confidence of any sort. But this morning, I have obviously been summoned by destiny.

It's a hot July day in the honking street. Buses are bumbling by. People everywhere, businessmen, moms dragging bags and kids. There's a calm looking guy in a Hawaiian shirt. I wonder if he's got a green garden by the sea on his home movie. Hard to imagine in this parking lot.

Suddenly the Skyler Building leaps a tall bound in a single slab, right in front of me. Wary of whiplash, I look up; these new ones are so tall. It's the newest glass tower overlooking the Financial District. Out front, a sculpture of steel spurts water out the top. It splashes down onto thin steel drums that boom quietly in response.

An elevator rises up the outside. The city to the east slips backwards in changing perspective as I ascend 100, 200, more than 300 feet up, looking down on the Music Center with mid-morning traffic snarled around it. I never did finish my cartoons.

On the 31st Floor it stops. The doors open into a wide room with grey carpet on the floor, purple lines running through it. No one's here. The sun's at my back through the floor to ceiling windows. Where's anybody?

The elevator door closes. I walk into the room. Consult my slip of paper. "3100, Skyler building. See Mr. Hugo."

I walk to the desk across the room where the receptionist should be. I look over the leading edge. A copy of Charles Dickens' "Hard Times" is open face down; a cigarette is burning in an ashtray.

A black-and-white security TV shows the street where I got in the elevator.

I turn around, look down a hallway; one door is open. I walk across the hall, into that door, into a smaller room. It's empty; there's a TV on the end of a slate grey table. Windows behind look north to the mountains, barely visible in the brown. The streets are a long way down. I always think about flying…or jumping.

A man on the TV is talking about the Bible. He looks like the type who would normally read stock news. I always talk back to TVs, why make an exception?

"Hello," I say in a jaunty tone: "Have you seen a Mr. Hugo anywhere?"

The man on the TV stops talking, looks very surprised and says to me, "Weeellll, very good. You are the very first one to come. I… am Mr. Hugo." He says it as if he knows I'll be impressed, then he almost starts laughing.

What do you do when a TV talks back? "Mr. Hugo? Really? Where are you?"

"I'm as near to you as I need to be, and as near as you need me to be. I can tell you this much, I have not been pre-recorded for broadcast in this time zone." He's just bubbling with enthusiasm.

He continues: "May I presume you have come in response to the advertisement?" Advertisement, as if he were English.

I swallow. "Ah, yes. Have you had many…other…applications? And, what's this all about, exactly? Where's my competition?"

"Oh, there is very little competition. We are very selective in our campaign," he says. "Then, of the even smaller number that actually come up here, you are the only one so far who has talked to the TV. You see, we decided to make that the test, and you have WON!" He laughs a jolly laugh. This guy probably does a great Santa Claus at the asylum.

Gulp. "Well, that's fine, but I am not sure I'm ready to save the world right yet.

"First, I have a few questions."

"We thought you might. Shoot."

"How many expenses are reasonable?" I like to cover the big points as soon as I can.

"That depends somewhat on how you plan to save the world, wouldn't you say?"

"Which brings me to my next question," I say. "How will you know the world has been saved?"

"Actually, we're somewhat open on that subject." Sounding a bit weary he says, "The world is a very complicated place. However, if you are able to convince us that you are trying very hard, and are getting somewhere, we may be satisfied. Of course, you will receive your expenses up front, because we do realize that this will be an expensive proposition. Can you give us an idea what you might require?"

"Welllll," I begin, reaching deep into my imagination. "As you might guess, I've given this a tremendous amount of thought, as have my compatriots"—I'm trying to imagine some—"of which there are now...well over...uh, 25...and each one of them will need...a minimum of $60 a day...as you can well imagine."

It's tough to tell from his face on the TV how he's taking this. I look for a camera, and finally find it looking at me from the top of the set. It does seem that he's looking down at me. Actually, he's looking down at the TV in his place...wherever that is. It looks like a bare room, pale walls. No clues. This is a strange situation I've walked into.

"Very good, Mr. Chris...Walkman, did you say? I'm very happy to hear that you have people you wish to work with, and, ah, draw energy from is how I like to put it."

The eye of the camera is like a stone. Hugo continues.

"If you will please look in the drawer over there, next to the radial reception machine, you will find $20,000. As you might guess, we're looking for really tremendous solutions to the pressing problems we all face in the world today, just name them. So, I want you to get out there and make a real difference, won't you? Everyone is depending on you.

"If you run into shortages of funds, please do come back and report how you're doing. We'll see about a possible second installment and discuss any special needs you may have."

He smiles his biggest, jolliest smile yet.

"Oh, yes: please don't go away with the money unless you plan to do something good with it. There's certainly more where that came from if you're making progress. For now, thank you very much for participating in our little program, and best of luck to you. We'll keep an eye on you." It sounds like a little song.

Then he zzzips into a tiny point of light on the screen.

I blink.

I walk over to the end of the table, next to the radial reception machine, whatever the hell that is. I pull open the drawer. There, indeed, is a bundle of $100 bills—200 of them I guess, wrapped just like in the movies with a little green band. It's just arrived from a slot inside the drawer, remotely activated. I consider reaching my hand into the slot, but decide not to. Probably steel knives inside. And the camera's still going, I bet.

But anyway, other things have begun to distract me in the room. Cherubim have suddenly appeared floating by my ears and a beautiful choir is singing religious music all around me. A hand has reached out of the sky and dubbed me "OK and ready to go" with a jet pack on my back and wings on my feet.

It's so nice to be chosen, to be considered for important work.

"But THIS IS CRAZY," I think, and the little cherubs pop into nothing. It's all quiet. The TV is blank.

Let's not get too excited. There are a few questions I could have asked, like who the hell the guy was, anyway. Twenty thousand bucks!

Then, another light begins to dawn. Skiing, heck! I think I'll start saving the world in Tahiti! They've got some bad problems there with coconut blight, I'm sure.

But no, nooo! This is seeeriousss. As I head for the elevator, the true nature of this moment is zooming in upon me. The last vestiges of my flippant attitude are transmogrifying. Why would I—humble I—have received this magnificent gift…unless, some person somewhere understands me at last? Someone, somewhere, has seen the potential lurking in the inner recesses, seen the racecar waiting in the dusty garage…until now.

I realize with a start that a young girl is sitting in the chair now, smoking another cigarette. She's maybe 25 and quite beautiful. I've seen her in my late-night dreams.

She says, "Goodbye Mr. Walkman" and gives a knowing smile that seems to recognize…that something in me.

"By the way, Mr. Hugo wanted me to tell you again that you shouldn't be taking off anywhere with the money. He feels sure you can make a very good start right here in California. OK?"

I'm positively insulted she would think I'd shirk on my commitment to making a difference, starting right here and right now. Tahiti! What a silly thought. No no no no no no no! We have serious things to do, right here in River City.

I start to wave goodbye with the most sincerely beatific smile I can muster. "And…," she says. I stop again.

"Mr. Hugo also wanted me to tell you that he knows you don't want him to report your little play action with the Pizza Place to anyone who'd want to know. But that's not going to be necessary, I'm sure."

"How did you know about that?" An icicle forms in the paradise.

"I don't believe the selection process is completely random," she purrs. "Anyway, that's not important, is it?" The voice is soothing and melts that mean old icicle clean away. I manage a decent version of a smile.

"Goodbye."

"Goodbye."

I ride down the elevator, out to the courtyard by the fountain. Droplets of water sprinkle my face, a gentle baptism. The booming sculpture is evocative of the coming of Roman troops far, far off, or of sounds in the womb.

Without really thinking, I've stuffed the money in my pocket. It makes a very big lump.

Not sure where to go, I walk east, away from the building. Faster and faster. A step full of life, a step that drives me forward with new speed, wings on my feet, the wind in my hair, and a song unspooling in the many screening rooms in the fun house:

"Hello my baby, hello m'honey, hello my ragtime gal!"

The frog is on the loose!

TWO

From up on Bunker Hill, I walk down to Broadway, a few blocks east. The hot press of people is overwhelming. Shoppers of many races wander into the doorways of stores where stereos blare. Tables are piled with dolls and toys, hats, shoes, books in Spanish and Chinese. Windows bristle with knives, sneakers, T-shirts.

In a daze, I buy a chili-dog at a stand, load it up with relish, onions, catsup, mustard, mayonnaise, just the way I love it. Makes the vegetarian in me feel better. Get a Coke too. It'll soothe my nerves.

The lump has turned into a fire in my loins. Don't dare touch the bills. Not yet. Not out in the open. Everybody's looking. Maybe they think I'm happy to see 'em, or they think I'm as weird as I feel.

Turn around, anybody watching me? Who can tell with the sidewalks so jammed? People are everywhere. These people should be making pyramids.

Walking slowly, I slowly eat, leaning forward so the chili doesn't drip on my shirt, Coke in the other hand, finally finish, roll up the paper tray in my hand, drop it in a trash box, by a table with magic wands on it.

It says "Magic Wands" right on the table—small hand-printed sign, a shallow box with maybe three dozen small metal sticks which I realize are actually ballpoint pens. They're cleverly done so that the jet-black shanks become silver tips. It says, "Magic Wand" right on the side. Why anyone would call it a magic wand I don't know. It does appeal to the budding artist in me.

The main thing is I'm dying to know if my new money is any good. Just for the fun of it, I'll make a purchase in bulk. Can't hurt. Maybe the pens will come in handy.

I look up the street, no one watching me. A man is walking towards me with his eye on the pavement. I look the other way; every one's walking with their back to me.

In the store, a man's leaning on the counter with his elbows and looking right at me. He stands up slowly, then walks farther back into the store and leans down, puts his elbows on the counter again, starts talking to someone. He's not paying attention any more.

I walk up to a broken penny weight machine for something to do. I'm not looking at anyone, I turn around, and reach nonchalantly into my pocket, looking into the machine. The bunch of hundreds is fully an inch thick. One single bill finally gets between my finger and thumb, and I slowly ease it out from the pack. Then I crumple it into a messy lump and pull my hand out of my pocket. Look up and down the street again. No one the wiser.

Suddenly, I'm looking at Benjamin Franklin, the man on the hundred-dollar bill. Never knew it was him on there. Jeez, like an omen. There are sure some heroes and favorite things in my life and good old Ben happens to be one because of the inventing and diplomacy and other good stuff he did. It's sort of a comfort to be looking at the old man all of a sudden, and on a hundred-dollar bill yet; I'm thrilled. Sure makes that bill look OK to me.

I take a breath and walk into the store with a substantial new source of inspiration in my hands.

"How much for the box of wands?"

The man stands up in the back. So does the other guy. They're just curious. "Great party favor. How much?"

"It says right on the box, $2 each." He leans over again on his elbows.

I say, "I'll give you $1.50 apiece for the lot. What's that, 50 bucks or something?"

The man walks slowly down behind the counter till he gets to the front of the store. He picks up the box.

"My friend, for 1.75 each, these are yours." He says "each" as if a parakeet had chirped. "They are all the way from Mexico City, and I have no more. What do you say, my friend?"

"Sold, if you've got change for a hundred?"

Sure, he doesn't even care. Sees it all the time. What a relief. The lump in my pocket has become quite a friendly lump.

We count out 38 magic wand pens from Mexico: $70.72 including tax. "Want a bag?" Sure.

I'm free. What am I going to do with 38 stupid pens? Expensive pens. I must be crazy.

It occurs to me I could use some smaller bills.

"Say could you change another hundred?" He does. Some people are really crazy.

OK, I don't know how one little frog can save the world, but might as well start at the bottom. For the fun of it, here's a hotel on Los Angeles Street.

Newspapers on the sidewalk are covered with grey dust. Neon sign, broken. A man with a frizzle beard, plaid shirt and baggy pants stares at me through watery eyes.

Why's he got brand new Reeboks on his feet? Latent enterprise, perhaps. "Hello, Sir," he wonders. "Could you lend me a dollar so I can eat some lunch?"

"What will you give me first?" I ask. "Will you tell me a story?"

He squints.

"Ok, tell you what." I pull out one of the magic wands from the bag. "Here's a magic wand that I believe can fix things. It helps you fix them yourself. See, it says magic wand right on here." I show him. He squints at it. "Tell me what I should do with it. I'll grant your wish."

He squints more and leans at me like he may be ready to lose his balance.

But I think he notices I may be crazier than he is.

"Make it give me some lunch," he says.

"That's your request?" I ask. I wave the wand over his head and say in a slow, serious tone: "You have the power to get your own lunch."

I can see he's not impressed. He reaches in his pocket and pulls out a hooked little knife just far enough for me to see.

"How's this for power?" he rasps.

I step backwards quickly and realize the fellow has perhaps missed my point.

The idea of the wand as an enabler is not clear to him.

"You've got the power to get your own lunch," I say again.

I put the wand back in the bag and start to walk away. Then I turn back, pick the knife out of his hand and toss it down the sewer. I drop the ballpoints, grab his wrists and look into his eyes. They are wide open. So is his mouth. He doesn't smell very good, and his clothes are stiff, but I believe he's starting to respect me. Thanks, Hugo and Ben, for the assist. I feel energy like just about never before.

I say, "Sir, I have a rule that says I never hurt anyone. I expect others to follow that rule, too." Not too sure where that rule came from, but you've got to have principles when you're saving the world.

"I'd like to make you an offer," I say, my significance growing. "It's clear that you would like some lunch, and some clean clothes. Am I right?" I'm really getting into this.

He gives a spastic little nod.

"Then let's take a quick shower—you, not me—get some lunch, then talk for a minute." He nods again.

We go into the hotel and up to the front desk. A shriveled man is sitting on a stool behind the counter. He looks at us; his head is bobbing on top of his neck like a toy dog.

"Can we rent a room for an hour?" I ask, then realize I may be giving a wrong impression. I muster a tone of disgust.

"He wants to take a shower," I say, pointing to the gentleman I'm holding. "Guess so," the man croaks. It's not much of a place, but he still wants $20 bucks.

"You do have a shower here, right?"

"Yep," the man croaks again. "Up in room 215, take the elevator or the stairs, be down here in an hour."

The walk up the two flights is an ordeal. It's a world down here I don't know at all. To say the least, it's alarming to me. Old men are sitting on the stairs looking half dead. Behind doors in the hallway, I hear a baby crying. Great flakes of paint are drooping off the walls.

We unlock the door at 215 and push it open. The floor of the place is painted brown. Great stains circle the ceiling.

The man heads into the bathroom where amazingly we find a piece of soap on the sink and a razor in the trash can.

"What's your name," I finally ask.

Speaking from still a long way away, he says "John." He's getting ready for the shower. I think I look like the Baptist. I sit on a chair in the room, thinking while the water runs. If this is the way to save the world, it's going to take a long time, one person at a time. That doesn't count getting food to people, and painting over all the graffiti. I stop thinking about the size of the job. It's what stops most people, I'm sure. With a wand from the bag, I scribble on a piece of paper.

Finally, John's ready, even though we haven't gotten new clothes yet. He's clean and clean shaven. A hint of self-respectability has crept over his face.

We go out of the hotel, for which I'm quite thankful. Aimless men in the lobby, old and young, black and white and brown, eye me suspiciously over their shoulders. A classic bag lady wheels her shopping cart along the sidewalk in front. This is a place of severe alienation. My job seems to get bigger and bigger.

I take John by the elbow, across the street to a greasy little restaurant where more men are stooping around. Bars cover the small windows of the restaurant. A 7-Up sign underneath advertises good cheer from another era.

At the lunch counter, my guest isn't talking much. Neither am I, but I never was much for small talk. I order a cheeseburger and a glass of milk for him. Forget it, no milk here. OK, gimmie a Coke, for him. John is still almost silent, says yeah.

He eats. My chili dog did me OK. I watch and draw some sketches on napkins. This one's supposed to be the Hotel Opportunity for people who don't know where to live, and they check in, get a bed and take a shower, get respectable looking and maybe we'll have Robin Seesman of the Psychological Difficulty and Clarification Institute talk to them all. Why can't they do some work like sweep or something in the rest of the hotel where other people stay cheap maybe? Takes too much money, I guess. And the unions would kill 'em.

Finally, we sit back in the cramped little booth. The restaurant is quite dark, but light from the door and window fills us in. I'm ready to make a pitch I've been formulating.

"If you could change your life and have anything you'd like, what would it be?"

I don't expect any B.S. What I get is silence. The new look of respectability has merged with a look of resignation, making him seem like a polite imbecile.

Where's the spark of enterprise I thought I saw? It was more than just the Reeboks, I thought. This is a strange new demeanor for the guy who threatened me so badly a while ago.

"Do you know what you want?" I ask.

He looks at his plate. It's clear now of perhaps the only idea he's had. Finally he looks at me again. He's been thinking.

He says slowly, seriously: "Since you asked. Here's what I'd like: a bed, a woman, a bottle of something great, and that's it."

I'm somewhat impressed with his coherence, but...

"That's it?"

"Sounds good to me," I agree, recalling my college days.

"Look," I say, "I've got this magic wand. Maybe you'd like another shot. What do you think?"

He looks that moron look.

"So what's your last name?" I ask.

"Fuller. John Fuller," he says. It's almost a growl.

"Like the brushes?" I envision the salesman who used to sit on our couch and show us samples from a suitcase. The memory brings more than a twinge of nostalgia.

"Yeah. I used to sell 'em. No relation."

"Why did you stop?" I ask,

"I wasn't very good at it; got lazy, drank too much. I ended up down here, on the Nickel. Haven't cared about very much for a while. Been surviving."

He looks at me and awareness has entered his eyes. He says: "What's our name, anyway?" sounding maybe a little bit suspicious, which is good.

"Chris Walkman," I say. "It's quite a story, but I've got a new job. I thought I'd try to help you out."

He just looks at me from across the booth. His suspicion is growing. Finally he says, "Thanks for the shower and the lunch. I'll see you," and he leans to get out of the booth, ready to slide out and back into the depths.

"I'd like to give you another shot, do you mind?" He stops and stares at the floor.

"Look, what's with this magic wand thing?"

"Just something I picked up. It's a prop. Let's give it another try."

"No thanks."

"But I insist," I say, propelled by I don't know what. It's a desperate cartoon move.

I leave money for our lunch on the counter and take him by the arm. We walk out the back door of the diner and I sit him down on a sunny box.

"Close your eyes, will you?" He's quite suspicious, looking at me sideways, but now he's resigned.

I take another wand out of my bag, maybe it's the same one. The sun reflects on the glossy black. It occurs to me this would be fun for kids. The cartoonist in me finds it satisfying, too. It does feel like a helper, for some reason.

I wave the wand over his head and say, "Somewhere your dream awaits—the bed, the broad, the bottle. Picture it now!"

He waits a moment, with his eyes closed. The lids cover his eyeballs like silk over fat marbles. Then he opens them, just a little bit wider than before.

I pause while it sinks in, whatever it was. For no particular reason, I'm vaguely satisfied. John obviously thinks this is entirely stupid. Hell, it didn't hurt him. Maybe he's amused a little, and the marbles have picked up just the littlest hint of a twinkle. Like I say, this save-the-world stuff is not easy. One person at a time, it's going to take a while. But I can celebrate small successes, can't I?

"Now, would you like a job?" I say. I'm trying to convey a new beginning and I'm really trying to make up some good stuff. That need to be creative runs deep in me, even though Ben Franklin would never do it this way, I know.

A new idea occurs to me. I say to John, "I could use a salesman. How about it? If you work hard, you'll do well."

I'm trying to turn on the charisma now. Sometimes it's there when I want it.

"What do I sell?"

"Contracts. And you can join the board of directors of a new company. In fact, I'm selling the first contract right now, to you, no cost other than your undying loyalty. While you sell contracts, or help out in other ways, I'll pay you $50 a day. OK?"

I think he's hypnotized, and it occurs to me that at the rates I set with Hugo, wherever he's sitting accounting for this expense, if he is, I'll make $10 bucks an hour profit on this guy.

"Here's a contract." I hold it out, a piece of paper I was writing on upstairs in the hotel, dribbling out some basic rules that seemed reasonable. I'm just making all this up, understand.

John looks at my big printed letters.

DON'T HURT PEOPLE.
HELP THEM IF YOU CAN.
RESPECT THEIR PROPERTY, AND YOURS.

"The bylaws of Magic Wand Industries," I explain, holding up the pen. "Now, let's add the stuff you want out of this deal."

The pen is poised. "What did we say?" I begin writing on the paper. This not neat, but I'm sure it's official.

"I, JOHN FULLER, AGREE MY MAJOR GOALS ARE TO FIND A WOMAN, A BED TO PUT HER IN WITH MYSELF, AND A BOTTLE."

I should probably be trying to up-sell him to a stiffer deal, but there'll be time to change the contract later.

I look at him. "That sound like it, more or less?"

He nods.

I hold up the pen. "Sign here, please, with your name and address. I'll do the same, as a witness."

I lay the scrap of paper down on the cardboard box, offer the pen. He takes it slowly, like it's moving through cold Jello and he might drop it. Then he signs his name, better than I expected actually. He looks up at me and says, "Where do I live now?"

"Why don't you come live with me for a while? 2020 West Morengo, West Los Angeles. OK? Got any better options?" He shakes his head.

Something maybe tender has entered his eyes. This changing the world stuff might work OK if the money holds out.

He carefully writes in the address, then gives me the paper, and the pen, one in each hand.

"Aright, John! We're set!" I clap him on the back, and a big cloud of dust rises off his shirt.

"Let's go!"

THREE

DAMN, DESPITE THIS SCREWED-UP frog of a personality, I think I've begun something important. Forget the Eiffel Tower.

While there's no reason to expect that my recruit, John Fuller, former brush salesman, will amount to anything, I've got his signed contract, and great hopes that maybe I've rescued somebody. That, and my new-found, Franklin-fueled courage drive me onward.

I have no idea what's next.

What time is it anyway? Just three. Alright, let's get looser and see what happens.

"John, you can earn your money. Who's the craziest person around here? I need someone with an imagination."

He's not used to thinking yet, but he reacts like he's coming around. He offers, "That would probably be Ivan Mann, the Russian artist. He's got a studio the other side of Los Angeles Street. You might like him."

"How do you know about him?"

"I've been here a while." He sounds almost proud of it. "I went to his studio once."

It's a relief to me that we leave Skid Row behind and walk farther east into the warehouse district. If I succeed in my mission, I'll be back here someday. There's a lot of people who need to be saved, badly. As we walk, John shows me stairwells he's slept in, restaurants that give out food and so on.

I could get very caught up worrying about this situation here. My cartoon visions that play on and on tell me there's got to be a way to get these people free, somehow. They're just sitting there. Why can't somebody just ask them to do something? Seems so simple!

Still, I have a feeling John will show scars for a long time. Right now, he's not entirely coherent and is saying some funny things. "Chris, I think you've been my best friend forever. I like that in the whole world." I'm touched by this.

John says his most recent bottle was this morning. I tell him I don't drink much at all and that I won't pay an employee who drinks. He says OK, but I'll believe it when I see it. Anyway, I'm sure drinking was only a fraction of his problems. Just living on the street makes you crazy.

We walk past a small crowd working on a bicycle of some sort. A bunch of vagrants are watching it being assembled. It's something like an ice cream vendor's tricycle with a cover over the top. I'm intrigued and I make John stop for a second, grabbing one of my pens to draw. Some guy's making a bicycle camper that somebody could sleep in; a bed folds down from the back, and there's even an alarm if somebody messes with it. It's a bicycle camper for the homeless, I gather. Now that is just my style. Because I like it, there's probably no way that thing's gonna catch on.

Finally, we arrive at what John indicates is Ivan's place. It's a glass front to a warehouse of some sort, with windows painted over in horizontal lines to suggest a video screen. I can just make out a man's face. Overhead it says "Museum of Mann."

I try the handle, the door opens. Inside is a showroom with some artworks scattered around on the concrete floor. It's obviously a gallery, walls painted white. A skylight washes it all with diffused sunlight. I love places like this because they make personal expression seem so…OK. I get inspired.

There's a table just inside the door with brochures and flyers from other shows, other galleries—sculpture, painting. I see that the annual Watts Towers Music and Arts Festival is coming up in two weeks. Idly, I pick up that notice.

John and I walk further into the studio. I smell new plaster. The sculptural pieces around us are probably supposed to do things, but I'm not sure if they're working at the moment.

"Hello!?" No answer. There must be a studio in back.

I walk up to the first piece—a thin stone slab with a roll of paper stretched across. A mechanical arm reaches out over the paper like an arrow and a sign on it says "Please indicate your state of mind here." A small part of the paper is awaiting my thoughts. There's a fat pen on a chain. Why not? I pick up the pen and write:

"The frog prince has come! Chris Walkman."

I touch a button that says, "Press when done" and a little printer puts the date and time on the paper by my words. July 14, 1991, 1:14 p.m. Then a winder moves the paper to the next frame. Blank space.

I say in a grand tone, "It has been noted: We passed this way; we exist!" John's just watching right now; he declines the offered pen, not ready to be noted yet.

Here's another work of Mann. A Polaroid camera is set up on a stand. It's pointing at a black-and-white grid and a little stool that a subject would sit on. A digital display at the top of the grid is broken; a hammer is smashed into the middle. On the back, several Polaroid images are arrayed neatly under glass, showing a monkey, a Neanderthal man and some people in period costumes. The last picture is Bart Simpson, the cartoon character. I gather evolution has stopped.

Another piece has got different colored handprints all over a framed piece of paper.

There are several TVs around in various displays. I wonder what's keeping them from walking out the front door. I call out, "Anybody here?!" No answer.

One TV is set into a large plaster eyeball. John and I are in it, looking at ourselves. A small camera is hidden above the TV. I think this must be "Candid Camera" day. Mr. Hugo's little show is fresh in my mind.

Frankly, looking at myself on the TV picture, I'm not impressed by what I see.

With my paunchy body and thinning grey hair, it's hard to believe I'm only 37. But next to me in the screen, making me look like a picture of health, John seems very thin and definitely needs some new clothes. Luckily, he'll probably be able to wear mine, which I'll arrange when we get to my apartment.

Looking at him, I suddenly realize he's fixed on himself as if he's shocked by what he sees.

"John, are you OK?"

He breaks his gaze at the TV.

"Yeah. I think you got me just in time, Chris." He looks back at his picture in the eyeball.

I like this art stuff. I get a picture of Ivan as technician and video artist using machines to mark man and his place in the cosmos.

Suddenly the back door opens up with a scrape on the floor. This must be Ivan in black pants, white shirt and a Dodger baseball cap.

"Who is here in my laboratory?" he growls in a great Bela Lugosi accent, with more than a hint of annoyance. Can't tell if he's really angry or not.

"Hello," I start, "we want to talk to you. John here says you've done some great things." I hesitate to use the C words—creative, or crazy.

"I don't want to be bothered right now. I'm working," he says, getting gruffer. He projects a lot of energy, definitely a temperamental Slovak. He's a short, thin man with what appears to be Napoleonic determination.

"I like your stuff," I say. "Can we talk about some things? I've got a new job and I'm wondering if you can help me."

He's suspicious.

"I enjoy your work here," I say again, gesturing at the room.

"Thank you," he says. Suddenly he brushes past us to the front door and locks the deadbolt with a sharp twist of his wrist. That explains why the TV's were unguarded. They weren't supposed to be.

Ivan sweeps back through the room and goes through the door he came out of, motioning us to come. John follows Ivan's quick moves, but very slowly. I follow behind, watching my charge.

We come into what does look like a laboratory. A pretty blond lady is sitting on the couch, watching us come in. She stands up and looks like she might greet us, but she stops and sits down again. Maybe she doesn't speak English. She says nothing, just looks at us.

Under high windows at the back wall of the studio, a workbench is littered with electronics and TV components. To the side, Ivan's got video editing equipment and shelves full of tapes, plus an audio mixing board. Somehow he's doing well. I'm excited at the array of resources staring me in the face.

What is apparently the current project is standing in the center of the room: two very large video screens built into large plywood frames, each about 10-feet high. There's black on the sides to conceal projection units inside, I guess. Lightning bolts decorate the tops and sides.

"They look very Nordic," I say to Ivan, though this may be a Thor point with him.

"It's a teleportation system," he says.

"Oh really?" I say, and then I'm embarrassed to sound so skeptical. It doesn't seem likely a miracle would be born in an L.A. warehouse, but one can always hope.

Ivan sees I'm doubtful. He says, "Let me show you."

He pulls black plastic curtains across the windows above the workbench and the room goes almost completely dark, though the sunny afternoon still peeks in around the edges.

Ivan leads John around to stand in front of one of the framed screens. Low ropes create a pathway that keep him from going too close or far away.

Then Ivan takes me over to the other screen, which is about 20 feet to the side. John looks sideways at me.

I notice that each screen has a camera mounted in front of it, right at the center, pointing at me and John. It's disguised to look like a ray gun or something.

Ivan is now ready and goes over to a pile of equipment where he grabs a master electronic switch just like the one Doctor Frankenstein used. He closes it with a dramatic flourish and lets out a cackle. I didn't realize he was actually cultivating this Bella Lugosi image. He rubs his hands together as he slouches back to stand beside me.

First comes a whine of electrical machinery, as if large generators are starting up. Vertical light poles beside each screen pulse with energy. Lightning flashes on the screen, explosions go off on the sound system like stage thunder, and puffs of smoke blow out of the floor where John and I are standing. This is a lot of fun.

Finally, some spotlights shine on me, at the same time as a life-size TV picture of John comes on the screen before me. I presume John sees me over on his screen.

The impression is quite good that John is actually standing there in front of me, behind a scrim of some sort. A faint grid is laid on the screen which helps create the effect of looking through a window. The small camera is not distracting.

I certainly get what Ivan's driving at. I turn to look at him and he's just picking up a sign that says, "Global Teleportation Inc." and fits it into the top of a stand next to us. The mad scientist is ready for business here.

"Ivan, I think your point is well taken. It's very real. The person almost gets here."

John is standing there just looking at Ivan and me. I can't see what I look like, only John.

"I like this, don't you?" I say to John. "Yes, Chris."

Bunches of ideas are occurring to me. I know that really I see this on TV all the time—news anchors talking to subjects on a screen by their desk. But I never see it full size. It's easy to forget how much TV is really transporting you someplace, even if it's just to a football game in Denver. Ivan's done a good job of reintroducing what TV does. This is really like looking at John straight on, especially because the camera allows for good eye contact.

I'm also thinking about all those commercials and videos we watch where the screen is alive with words and fast edits, and we just sit there passively watching, absorbing while the stuff pours in. I see all those couch potatoes out there. It's not that it's a big issue with me, necessarily, but now that I'm saving the world, I think I deserve to be little more self-righteous.

This helps you think of TV as a different thing.

"John, think of the distances we can cover and still be face to face. What if people used TV to really talk to each other?" He nods. Can't tell if he's thinking about it or not.

"By the way, John, you need some of my clothes, pretty soon."

"Thanks, Chris that would be nice."

"Watson, come here, I need you!" I laugh at my own joke, recalling the first words Alexander Graham Bell said on the telephone.

"Nice work, Ivan. Lot of ideas in this thing. Are you going to take it to the shopping malls?"

"I have no such ideas," he says with some indignation. "This is a gallery piece. The idea for me is to show people to themselves on the screen and beside each other, as we are here. It would cost too much to cover long distances with satellite or whatever. Obviously you could connect places."

"It would be quite popular I bet."

After a beat, I say, "Ivan, you don't know me from anyone, right?"

"That is right, but I have seen your friend down here before."

"Oh, I'm sorry. Ivan, this is John. John brought me to you, Ivan. I asked him who was crazy down here and he immediately suggested you."

Ivan laughs and looks at John. "Thank you for the compliment, John. And may I introduce Petra, there on the couch. She is being shy today."

The woman has been watching us. She stands up now straight and stiff, stretching her legs. Then she sits down again on the edge of the couch and says, "Hello." She continues to project an intense, reserved feeling.

"Hello," I say. She's quite interesting…but clearly spoken for. My high principles cause me to turn my head back to Ivan quickly.

"Ivan, I know you have no reason to trust me, but I would like to offer you a contract. It's one that John here agreed to today, very simple, and I think…"

"I don't do contracts," Ivan interrupts.

"I believe it's a good one," I say, trying to be earnest, working up the charisma.

Not much is coming because this guy is out to resist me, and I don't usually do well with resistance. Then I remember I'm Franklin-powered.

"Allow me to explain. First, I don't want to steal your system here or any of your ideas. The contract should make that clear. Second, you might be able to use me. Third, I'll pay you $50 a day."

Ivan and Petra both let out loud snorts. Oh Benny, don't fail me now!

I say, "Look, I'll write out a copy of the contract right now. Can you give me a piece of paper?"

"You seem to have forgotten some minor details," Petra says. "What is YOUR name and what are you intending to do? Why do you want a contract?" She has stood up from the couch and is walking over to Ivan and me.

"Ah, yes...that's funny. Minor details!" I'm starting to get flustered.

"My name is Chris Walkman. I guess I should explain that I've just gotten a new job today, which is that I'm doing my best to save the world. I'm looking for people who can help, and I think a contract will unite us better. Happily, I can compensate you for your time."

They all are suddenly looking at me in a very tight sort of way, studying me for cracks in my sanity. Even John didn't really hear this before."

"Saving the world?" Petra says.

To slake some of their curiosity, I say "Sorry, I can't discuss details of my employment much further, but I do have the wherewithal to make some things happen. Are you interested in helping?"

Petra says, "To save him the embarrassment of telling you himself, you should know that Ivan can make 10,000 dollars a day directing rock 'n roll music videos.

Your offer strikes us as low."

This is more food for thought. She must be the agent or something. "Yes, but how often does Ivan get a chance to save the world?"

"His work has its satisfactions."

My eyes scan the three faces—Ivan, Petra, and John's, still on the video screen.

I know almost nothing about any of these people, but for some reason I think we'd make a good team. That's not an expert opinion, of course.

"I'm not sure how to convey the fact that I'm serious. Will you join my team? I'm thinking of some things we can do together."

She says, "Such as...?"

I'm casting about, wanting to be ready with a creative thought. My mind goes to the Watts Towers Music and Art Festival flyer still in my hand.

"What about this?" I hold it up. They read. John comes over, too. "Right in town here we can link to something that's fun, bust through a membrane out there between two separate worlds, see what happens."

I'm rushing into something awful fast. But this seems like a great idea and really creative people trust their instincts, I know that.

"Ivan, and Petra, I'm in a mood to try things out, and Ivan, you seem like just the guy to help. Your system here looks like a great way to do something different. I can at least pay expenses."

To reinforce the point, I carefully pull out the money pack from my pocket and hold it up. All three mouths drop open a little bit and the eyes get wider. I'm happy to be making a stronger impression, but I feel more than a little bit exposed. I'm afraid the money is about all the credibility I've got in the world at the moment.

"I don't do this just to impress you. But I do hope you'll take me seriously.

"Now what about that contract?" I put the money back in my pocket.

Ivan looks at me, then at John, then at Petra. He walks over to the workbench and grabs a piece of graph paper and a pen. He stops and looks at Petra again. She really must be the agent. She's looking at him, poker-faced, but he really studies her. Then one arm sticks out and he gives me the paper and the pen. He's still looking at her.

I give him back his pen, and carefully pull out a magic wand pen from my sack.

"Pardon me if I use my own. These have come to have quite a bit of significance to me." I look at John who says nothing.   I write the same words that John read, about not hurting people and so on. I think this whole thing is an important step. All my days of cartoons tell me so.

After reading, Ivan says, "I like the part about respect property. My art is my property." He waves around at the studio. "I copyright every damn thing I can, state my claim. I learned this in my country, where the lack of such protection was our undoing."

"Ivan, write down the things you want," I say.

"I certainly will," he says. "First, I retain any copyrights, patent rights and so on that may come up in anything I do, including the Global Teleportation System. Second, I am not your employee, but your partner. Third, I have the installation contracts if we do more with this system, wherever they may go."

I'm impressed, but unconcerned about those details. "Sounds great. Write 'em in. Mostly, Ivan, I need your ideas. I think we can make a great show with your system and connect people in a new way."

John nods his head. It's a little sign of support, but it means a lot to me.

Petra stands behind Ivan and puts her chin on his shoulder. There's still tension here, but I'm even more convinced it's a good group.

"Petra, I'm pleased to meet you," I say, trying to win her trust. "Where are you from?" She's much less uptight. Maybe she's decided I'm OK, and that's a good thought, too.

"Nova Scotia. My dad was a fisherman. I've been here for a few years. I love the ocean." Then she says, "You still didn't tell us much about yourself. Where are you from? What do you do?"

"I'm an animator. I'm hoping we can animate some people with Ivan's good system."

"Ready when you are, weird partner," Ivan says.

I hope that's a term of endearment in the old country.

FOUR

Watts. South Central Los Angeles.

You might think of electricity, but mostly the city is a short circuit. It's a hotbed of gang activity and one of the poorest black communities in the country.

Used to be that Watts was separate from Los Angeles, not so caught up in the megalopolis. Nice families lived there—Black, Hispanic, and Anglo. The Pacific Electric Red Cars once stopped there on their way to San Pedro. Now the Blue Line does, going to Long Beach. It opened some time ago, the first new commuter rail in L.A. for decades.

I'm here now because of Sam Rodia and his towers. He's another one of my heroes, along with Ben Franklin.

Rodia was an Italian construction worker who moved to Watts in 1921 or thereabouts. He's sort of a myth now, hard to pin down. Bought a triangular little lot with a house on 107th Street. He had something big on his mind.

Maybe he was just devoted to the monumental, but for whatever reason, just after he came here, he began a 30-year process. It seems like he knew just what he wanted to do when he started, and then did it.

He walked around looking for pieces of civilization—bits of broken crockery, glass, tile, silverware, and shells. Far as I know, he always worked alone. But gradually he built from the flatness of his yard three steel reinforced towers, the highest almost exactly 100 feet tall, and four smaller pinnacles. He covered them with grey cement and the colorful tile. The Watts Towers are a true piece of folk art.

To me, what he did is much, much better than bungee jumping off the Eiffel Tower. The towers have lasted. People like me come to see them because they stand for something—what one man can do, even when he's a poor immigrant. They look like a science fiction machine that draws rings of power right out of the ground and into the sky.

In 1959, the city decided the towers might be too unstable to leave standing.

They decided to do a test, attaching some ropes to the top like a lynching of old. The tension on the ropes was increased, to 10,000 pounds. The engineers cleared a space for the monument to fall... and it didn't. The testing machinery gave way first.

The engineers took off their hats afterwards, wiped their brows, and looked up again at the work of a madman who one day decided his towers were finished, and disappeared. His work remained.

To me, the inlaid surface looks like our society reassembled from fragments.

Rodia was definitely a cartoonist of the first order.

Ivan, Petra, John and I finally agreed it was a good idea to conduct an experiment in connecting people right here in the shadow of Rodia's towers.

Most people think of Watts as the Watts Riots of 1965. The community has had lots of money poured in since then, but has still not really recovered. Many kids have no idea what work is. They've never considered even looking for a job. I can relate, actually.

Today, Saturday, July 27, 1991, is the Watts Towers Music and Arts festival. The event is being put on by the Art Center here. They said, come on down and join us. Now, music and drums sound from around the little park next to the Towers. The smell of spicy food and barbecues fills the air, drives me crazy. People are everywhere, enough to make our communication here worthwhile.

We've assembled our gear on the lawn just outside the steel fence that surrounds the Towers. Blue Line trains zoom by a block away. Their horns are quite piercing, even at this distance.

Petra has come with me, to help work Ivan's projection system, which she turns out to know very well. Ivan and John are 20 miles across town, on the edge of UCLA in Westwood. We debated a while where to go, but that seemed distant enough in concept, with many people there on a Saturday night. I could have been over there, but this area seemed more exciting, and I was drawn to the towers.

However, I'm very aware that the Crips or the Bloods gangs are also part of this community. It's almost 7 p.m. as I look at my Kermit watch. I'd like to be gone by 9 when the shooting starts. I didn't say I wasn't nervous.

But it's just that sort of fear that makes breaking through from Watts to L.A. seem like an excellent gesture, and Ivan's system looks like a great way to do it.

Working with Ivan the last two weeks, I've been knocked out by what a talent he is. You'll see. He's made this possible, plus his screens, his cameras, recording equipment, his P.A. system, and some great video footage he's collected.

We've rented portable microwave dishes and a truck, and I was lucky not to use all the money. I've been meaning to get back to Hugo. I'm paying Ivan and John and Petra the $50 a day, plus rental for his stuff. He's been very reasonable. So has she. They're really boosting my confidence as we bring this particular cartoon to life.

I'm amazed we could barely get any TV station interested, which would have been a great extension of the idea. KWIL Channel 8 told us to bring by some footage later, we'll see.

It's just after sunset, and the smog is trying to justify itself, coloring the horizon with an alarming shade of orange against the deepening blue. Time to test our microwave link. It worked yesterday. I say a little prayer it works because at these rental prices, I can't afford to do this more than once, unless Hugo is impressed. I haven't got much to show him yet, otherwise. I'm pissed about those TV stations.

"Petra, can we talk to Ivan? It's time."

She's been checking wires to the projection screens, P.A. speakers. She comes over to the rented van where I'm looking at the equipment inside.

She moves in close next to me, quiet, but I can tell she's excited, too. "Chris, are you ready for surprises?"

"Petra, that's why we're here! Courage…and let the show begin!"

She flips some switches. We look at a small TV monitor. It cones on and there is Ivan in the parking lot just up from the Mann's Theater in Westwood. It's right by UCLA. He comes over to the camera and looks at us. He's looking, too, at his screen. John is right there next to him.

Things are not aligned for viewing eye-to-eye on the monitor. That will only work with the big screens. But Ivan sees me. The microwave link is working, and I can barely talk with excitement.

"Hello, Ivan, John. This is incredible. Ivan, you're amazing!"

"Hello, Chris. We can see you here on this monitor quite well. It looks like Petra and you have done a good job setting up. We're already here. I should say we can start."

I look around again at the screens that Ivan had set up in his work room.

They seem more fragile out here in the night air. The projectors are enclosed in the black tents behind the screens.

I finally say, with less conviction than a fearless leader might convey: "OK, let's go!"

A crowd has gathered—revelers with hotdogs and African shirts, plus tough black kids with Reeboks and dirty T-shirts, some with bandanas.

"Hey man, whatcha watchn? Hey dude, that's cool. Gonna play some music?

"The speakers look pow-er-FUL! Let's see some rappers!"

I should have thought of that and played some rap music, but there's been plenty today at the Arts festival. That would have really got the people moving. I put a light on the kids and the rest of the crowd for visibility, and turn on the show. The thunder rolls, the explosions rock, the smoke jumps out of the floor pipes. And, bang, on the screen, there's a crowd of white folk in Westwood, startled by the start-up.

They are curious. Their projection screens have just come on, too, and they are looking at the black folks, who are returning the favor.

"Who's that?" says a fat guy in a Mickey Mouse T-shirt on the screen from Westwood. He's talking to a girl next to him. They might be on their way to a movie. Twenty miles away, it seems much farther in concept.

A large black lady comes up near me, on my end of the city. "Where is he? Where are those people?"

"They're in Westwood, ma'am," I say. "You can talk to them if you want to."

"I can?" Sort of a shriek voice, but there's good humor in there. "How did I do it?

"Ask him what he's doing in Westwood tonight." "Yeah?" That shriek. She turns to the screen. "Hey you, hey Mr. Mickey Mouse."

The man looks side to side to see who spoke. The woman says, "Yeah, you, with the Mickey Mouse."

He looks at his shirt, looks at the screen, at the image of the black woman he's just seen and heard talk to him.

"Me?" He pushes his fingertips into his ample stomach as if to identify himself.

"Yeah, you. I guess I'm talking to you. Where you at?"

"Me? I'm in Westwood. Where are you?"

"Heck, I'm down here in Watts," she says in her siren tone. She's taking command.

"Look at them folks," she says to the people near her. "They in Westwood." She says to me, "Ain't that right. You said they in Westwood, right?"

"That's right, and you heard the man say it, too."

"So what is this thing? How come I can talk to them? Did you do this?" She doesn't even pause and begins talking again to the man in Westwood.

"Who's that wit'cha? That your wife?"

He, too, has been talking to people there, and now turns back to her, "Yes, this is my wife, Alice. We're going to see 'Dangerous People,' the movie. How about you, what's your name, and what are you doin' tonight?"

"We're at a party!" she says. "Come on over."

"Seems like we did already," he says. Good point.

Kids on skateboards gather around him, looking at us too, calling things to themselves and us. It's good they can't see themselves on TV, it would be a big distraction.

Ivan appears on the screen for a moment.

"Hello, Chris," he says, though I'm not in front of the screen. I can see John standing in the crowd next to a woman. We're up and running, I give Petra a little hug. Ivan disappears.

"You're at the Watts Towers, aren't you? I can see that," says the man. "What's goin' on there? Who else is there?"

"My kids," the woman says. She looks around. "Abe, get over here." The siren pulls a youngster by the ear. "Talk to the man."

"Hey fatso, wha's happ'nin," says the youngster. The lady smacks the kid on the back of the head.

The fat man says, "Sheeeet," and looks ready to leave.

I stand there, just enjoying this for a while. People on both sides figure out quickly they can talk between the two places as if it were a hole in the fence, like the Berlin Wall broken through. I think it's miraculous, even though it's something TV could have done and did do 50 years ago. Not out here, though, not on the street. The view before us could be across a sidewalk. The space between us doesn't matter anymore. The conceptual fence is getting just a little bit thinner.

I don't think a TV documentary would do this.

Some musical acts come perform in front of the screen as well. An African dance troupe of ladies and men does a frenzied dance to drums. A blues singer captivates people all by himself. After almost an hour, the focus of the entire party has turned to our screens, a real crowd's here, maybe 1,000 though certainly not everyone can see very well. Good we put out some extra TV monitors away from the front.

Hard to tell how big the crowd is in Westwood.

People are having a great time. Frankly the division between the races—black to white—seems almost irrelevant, and actually Westwood is much more ethnically mixed than I expected.

Basically, people are having fun. There's more bad language than I expected.

It's funny, too, the way some people hang around the edges, then gradually work their way to the front of the crowd and take center stage.

A black kid does that in Westwood. The big black lady says, "Hubert?! What are YOU doing THERE?"

I decide it's time for our show. I walk over to Petra, tap her on the shoulder. She's been watching. I nod, it's time. She goes to take a prearranged station by the door of our van, ready. Smoothly I pick up the microphone from a table in front of me and take a big breath.

"People," I call out in my most commanding voice. "May I have your attention please?" The bustle quiets only slightly even though Ivan's sound system is great.

"My name is Chris Walkman," talking very slow so no one will miss a word.

"I will start by saying that I am quite pleased you are all here tonight. Do you enjoy our Global Teleportation System? And for you lucky folks here in Watts, how about a hand for the Music and Arts Festival. Great!" People clap.

"Hey man," someone calls from Westwood, "are you Phil Donahue?" What a low blow, I think to myself.

"I work for a lot less than Donahue," I call out. Where's some patter when you need it? "And I'll even talk to you!" I guess I should have expected hecklers.

"You know, it's evident to me that much is wrong with the world today. Does anyone disagree?"

No one does. Suddenly people look like stones. I've invaded a party.

"I mean, take this gap—you here in Watts, talking to the people in Westwood. It's an enormous gulf, between rich and poor. Don't forget your fear…of the gulf we are bridging here tonight.

"But see how easily we cross it? I've listened to your talk. It's easy, it's friendly. Face to face, we are all just people. We can converse. Yet, who in Westwood would come to visit Watts? And is it easy here in Watts to think of such an escape? Why must this distance between us exist?"

It's quiet, at least. I can't tell if I'm getting to anyone. I look at Petra for some support. She smiles a whisper.

"I think there is a block between people. Even while we party tonight, I know you people are afraid of the gangs around, even though many of them are your children, your brothers and your sisters. They are shooting each other, across borders of their imagination…from territory they think they must defend, when, really, there is no threat.

"Why must this be? Where did the need come from to define such borders, when really, no borders exist?

"It's people drawing lines against each other…as natural and as sad as war, I suppose."

"But we all know the gangs are merely symptoms of far deeper problems, of the poverty and fear among the races that has poisoned our society for generations.

"I'm here tonight to ask what we can do to address these concerns, despite their stranglehold on our dreams."

I pause.

"Pollution." I look at Petra, who has already moved to turn on our tape of some material that Ivan's helped prepare.

The tape shows the beautiful ocean, then a beach with dead birds and waste.

The screen dances with images of our environmental madness. Smoking factories. Choked freeways. For a few minutes now, I'll be tied to the unwavering timeline of a prerecorded tape, speaking to changing images on the screen.

Deliberately, I drone a hypnotic drone.

"Again, we create borders…between ourselves, and our planet. One day our industrial engine will soon burn us out. Fossil fuels will render us unto fossils before our time.

"Day by day, we corrode the very air we breathe. Our life blanket is being frayed and soon we will be naked before a storm."

Petra is ready with a camera on my face, which now appears larger on the screen, here, and there in Westwood. Another tape recorder is slowly winding, catching it all.

A quiet pause, and traffic murmurs in the background. People crane necks to look over the back of the crowd.

"Let me tell you a story now, and listen. Begin with me, right here…in your imagination." I touch my head.

41

Now Petra and Ivan with cameras catch faces in the crowds—still and serious, suspicious but watching.

"Look at yourselves. Two societies in one city…a city, in fact, of many societies, many gulfs in our understanding.

"Imagine for a minute what you already know…that we are not different societies, but one. Step back in your mind and picture our shared home—our earthly spaceship."

The pictures of the crowds blend, then fly back into a green prerecorded landscape. That image in turn recedes and becomes the earth in space. Ivan is doing some great editing on the fly all the way over in Westwood. The pre-recorded vision looks into a sky full of stars, to moving comets of blazing light. Once again, the pictures match my words, which I speak from careful memory as the pictures appear.

"Fly with me silently into space and watch as OUR earth recedes into a blue-green sphere…a cat's eye marble…a speck. Then, the earth is gone and only we in our imaginations are left…floating amid the planets, then out beyond the sun. We are a phantasm of energy lost in infinity.

"One day, my friends, that will be all that's left of us. A distant cosmic memory."

The sound of wind whispers from the speakers, trying to suggest the infinite. No one's yelling, at least. Now I need the best Martin Luther King voice. If only I had it.

"But WHAT IF this memory IS ALIVE, out there in our future? What if this

Cosmic memory of us IS ANGRY…Angry at the waste of if all…Angry that our home was burned, our life snuffed out by greed, that people died in poverty and despair. Imagine that this angry memory of what we could have been NOW HAS A FORCE OF PURPOSE and no boundaries in time? It wills a return, flying in an instant, past the planets, towards the earth, RETURNING TO ITS SOURCE."

Ivan's excellent images suggest all this, and I think it works. Trying to radiate energy and confidence, I look slowly around at the gathered multitudes and continue.

"EVEN NOW, THIS FUTURE MEMORY...OF OUR HOPE TODAY...

IS RETURNING INTO OUR MIDST. AND FROM ITS ANGER...FROM OUR SI-£AME...THE MEMORY OF US...HAS FASHIONED A NEW RESOLVE.

"Before your eyes, this new hope...IS MADE REAL!"

Petra and John time the lights just right, which burst on in a fierce glow into the people's faces. A soundtrack on the videotape plays a big harmonic chord.

Caught in the light at both locations, surrounded by the crowds, are two silver wheels, shimmering like snowflakes, spokes radiating from their centers. These are supported by invisible wires which make them look like they are floating. Our show is working perfectly.

"The force of our shame has returned as hope. It presents itself now to those who will welcome it.

"Know this force as The Wand."

I have walked over to the wheel, lit by our well-placed spotlights. So has Ivan, I hope, though I can't see him because the lights have now washed out the screens.

We both reach to the top of our wheels and pull out a single spoke, one of my ballpoint pens wrapped in silver paper.

Ivan and I, after careful rehearsal, now recite in unison, in our separate places:

'The Wand is a force...for writing and picturing your ideas for good and for hope. Take it all of you who would change the world. It delivers a power you already possess...to express your own worthy visions for a better life on earth." I sure hope this is going to hit people right. This is our big gamble.

"To have it, and enjoy this power, there is only one thing we ask. Sign this contract everyone."

We hold up the small pieces of paper.

Now I try to return to a more normal voice: "You will be partners in Wand Enterprises. If we need your services, you will receive 50 dollars each day. In return, we ask only that you abide by the terms of our agreement.

"The contract says this.

"One, do not hurt people. "Two, help them if you can.

"Three. Respect their property, and yours.

"And to that you will add your own ideals and commitments as they are appropriate to you.

"With this and The Wand, WE will change the world. Your ideas are yours to act upon…or, send them to Wand Enterprises at the address on the contract." That's the official Wand Enterprises headquarters, my apartment.

"Everybody, here and in Westwood: to make a difference, starting right now…

COME ON DOWN!"

I couldn't resist that end. I knew we'd be descending to chaos at this point anyway. What the hell.

We have 200 wands at each site, which I managed to pry out of my good friends back in the store on Broadway. They found another full box. Our crowds are big, but I don't expect that many takers at each place. These people know I'm crazy now.

"What is that…wand?" says young Abe.

"It's a magic pen," I say, "to help you write down and make up your own new ideas." His mother is pulling him back, but he yanks free.

"You a bunch of jive talk," he says to me, "but I want one of those. When do I get my 50 bucks?"

'Tonight, kid, "I say. I've got a job for you. Sign here. You too, ma'am?" I look at his mother.

"No-oo sir," she says.

Abe pulls away and takes a contract and a pen from me. Mom shakes her head. The boy can barely write his name, but he does. I take the paper, give him his original copy and place the carbon in the records box. Petra is helping the others, so there are a few other copies there already. The music has resumed in the background and I'm moving and grooving to the rhythm as I talk to people. I am totally high on the way this thing is turning out.

"What about my wand?" Abe says. His voice has a demanding tone, which I like.

"Come with me my boy." I am W.C. Fields as a master showman; I take his hand and place it above a wand, right at the top of the wheel. His fingers close gently on the end. He lifts the wand out of the wheel's hub. I can tell instantly it's having the desired effect. Abe looks at me; the cynicism in his eyes is gone, at least for a minute.

"What's your full name?" I ask, more serious. I want to remember this kid, even if I never see him again.

"Abraham. Abraham Lincoln," he says. It's so corny at this moment it makes me smile.

As we get it all packed up, only a few wands are left. As I expected, the great majority of the people walk away. Either they can't bring themselves to come up, or they fully understand how crazy I am.

The people who do sign up we make a point of sending to the screen so they can introduce themselves to sign-ups at the other site, and to the ones here, too. I honestly am not sure what comes next with this group, but it seemed to be a good idea to do this. Who knows what kind of a team we might end up with? Wand Enterprises is a big idea about ideas that I hope will grow.

The exciting thing to me is that some people get it right away.

One young woman with a boy in her arms comes up and says to me, "Sir, I think tonight is a great thing you're doing. I got two boys, and one's gangbanging' already, and he's 11. This one here is 4 but he's gonna be into it, too. I got this idea, would you listen?" The sadness really comes through.

"Ma'am, I'd be proud to listen."

"Well, I think maybe we need to get the National Guard out here, you know.

But not like the riots. Make it more like boy scouts or big brothers or something really strong that kids can join, and get those soldier guys to be like something' to look up to? My husband's gone. My girlfriends are in the same boat with kids and the daddies gone. My kids need something good to look up to. You understand? You know what I mean. Is that a good idea?"

"That's great." I wish I knew how to do it or where to tell her to go with people who are trying it already, like Big Brothers or whoever it is. I guess my job is to think what comes next, and be a resource.

"That's great. Put that in, will you. We'll try to figure what comes next. I want to help. We really want to help." I sure feel like I'm taking on a lot.

She says thanks, and heads back into the crowd. The boy looks heavy in her arms. I just picked up some of his weight.

Many people continue to stand around in conversation between kids here and kids in Westwood. I can see that John and Ivan have reduced their wheels to almost nothing as well, and are sending many people to the screens to talk. It's been satisfying evening—just about as planned—even better than cartoons—sort of like cartoons in fact. One of the cops here in Watts even took a wand and signed up. He thought it was all silly, which it certainly is, but heck, the Wand stands for something good. Some people can relate to that.

The promises of money for work—honestly I don't know where I'm going to end up with that. That makes me tired, too. It'll mean a trip to see Hugo very soon. And that is going to be a very important conversation. I hope I can play him the tape we've recorded tonight. But these souvenirs, and the $50 a day, all this equipment rental, these things have really added up. After I settle up the rental, I know what I'll be left—about $1,000—not much commission for me.

Abe makes his first $50 helping to stow away our gear. He wants to go with us, but his mother won't have it. He did get her to sign up, though.

"How am I going to know where to find you," Abe asks.

"I'll find you," I say. It's what I'm telling everybody. I'm not sure what else to say. Really, everybody who signed up wants to know how they can make their 50 bucks. One guy wanted a raise. I told them all I'd get to them as soon as I needed to. I hoped it would be soon, I said. I hope I'll think of a really good reason.

FIVE

WHAT COMES NEXT IS just more making it up.

Ivan, John, Petra and I meet as planned at the TV station KWIL in Hollywood, at 9:30. After their vaguely expressed interest in seeing some of our event in Watts and Westwood, I'm hopeful they will air something. It could be a great way to extend the launch of Wand Enterprises.

Petra and I arrive first in the rented van full of extra equipment and the microwave link. About a minute later, Ivan rolls up in his car, a beat up Camaro with a trailer full of his gear. To my surprise, right behind is a little Pinto. Out climbs John from one side, and a little lady with curly blond hair and a big smile out of the other side. They slam the doors. He's still the Jello man, moving slow like an ocean liner. Where'd he meet the lady? Then I realize she's the one I saw him standing next to in the broadcast, the window I'm going to call it.

"Hello John. Hello Ivan!" I think we've become old pals in two weeks it feels like, but they never looked better to me. I spread my arms out wide and give them each big hugs.

Ivan says in his thick voice, "I must congratulate you on something quite interesting, Mr. Chris. I honestly do not know where you will take this thing, but you led us to an interesting beginning." He's rocking back and forth all the while. Energy got into him, too.

John comes up and is right away polite: "Chris, this is Judy. She plays piano and was nice to offer me a ride. Judy, meet Chris Walkman, the master of our invention tonight."

"Oh, no," I say. 'That honor belongs to Ivan over here, our video craftsman." I'm trying to keep the team spirit as high as I can. "And Petra, well done."

She's still got fiery eyes, but I think they look happy. Certainly, they made enough money off me, they ought to be happy. But I'm not dragging that out in the open.

Ivan gives Petra a squeeze of the shoulders. She jabs him in the stomach.

True affection among life boxers.

I look back at John. "More impressed with the Wand than ever, I bet," giving a full glance at Judy to emphasize my meaning. He just smiles. For a guy who was so angry before, tried to slice me before, he sure turned into a pussycat. The Jello pussycat.

We walk into the glass-walled lobby of the station. I listen to our feet scraping on the concrete. My ears are tuned like a bat's. The place smells like old roses for some reason—air freshener probably.

At the desk, a guard is reading the sports section. He looks up as we walk toward his desk, the five of us. We all feel pretty weary. He's not overwhelmed with delight to see us either. He tips his head to the side, and makes a funny squinty wince, as if he's trying to focus better.

"Can we speak to the weekend news director, please?" I say, and consult a piece of paper. "Janda Evers."

"She's in a meeting. And we're closed," he says.

"It's not closed," I observe. The TV behind him shows the 9 o'clock news is underway. I'm leaning on my elbows as far over the counter as I can, so I can smell his cigarette breath.

"Why do you want to see her?" asks the vigilante.

"Sir, you are being very rude. In fact, I have an appointment with Miss Evers. We have with us here some outstanding footage of an event that happened tonight SIMULTANEOUSLY in Watts and Westwood. We formed a corporation with people from both areas that could change the world." I'm still high on this thing, and I'm not used to success of any sort, you understand.

The fellow winces some more. After all our preparations for the big event, I guess I should have a better plan for what comes next. But I feel sure the station will make a story out of this material, extend the impact. No thanks to the Cyclops here.

He looks at me some more, and picks up a phone, talks quietly down the mouthpiece, hangs up.

"Please sit," he says. I'm beginning to warm towards the guy, the way I might to the arctic sun.

We all go sit on the couches and look at each other. I realize we're all pretty emotional and tired. I could be in a dream. My indoor movie theater keeps running instant replays of faces I talked to, the lights coming on, the spoked wheel of Wands, and the delicious self-satisfying sound of my own amplified voice. I guess I'm drunk, if you want the truth. I almost worry about coming down.

Net to me on the couch, John's muttering to Judy who keeps up this silly smile all the while. I'm just looking around when one of the most beautiful women I have ever seen strides out of a door. She's very tall with a great face and long brown hair. Wearing fashionably baggy green pants and a black blouse.

"Hello, I'm Janda Evers. May I help you?" She looks from one to the other of us, seeking me, I guess. I'm the guy who called.

"Hello, Janda," I stammer. My breath is almost gone. "I'm Chris Walkman." She reaches out her hand and we shake. I introduce the others, and Judy, who smiles.

"I talked to someone on the news desk this week and they said you might be willing to see our footage from a production we did tonight simultaneously in Watts and Westwood."

As evidence, I point to the two videotape cassettes that Ivan is holding—two tapes, one for each screen in the two locations.

"Yes, Chris, I'd be happy to take a look. Unfortunately, given the time, we probably can't do anything tonight. Our show is pretty much in the can. Frankly, I'm sorry no one referred you to me earlier. As I understand the concept, it's interesting. I've been looking for unusual things like this."

Imagine my delight. Jesus H. Christ where *was* she before! Petra rolls her eyes. I suddenly think I must look like an idiot to these pros.

Janda says, "Please follow me, everyone."

We start to follow her long strides as she leads us back to an edit bay to view the tapes. John hesitates, then indicates he's going to say goodbye to Judy who's apparently going home. There is a wistful look on his face. I stop to shake her hand.

She beams, "You were all very impressive this evening. The people in Westwood were still talking when we left. All sorts of people came up to John with ideas and they all wanted to know when your thing might come back. Is it? Are you going to do it again someday?"

"I certainly hope so," is all I can say. The funds factor is top of my mind on that point.

"Well, I do too," Judy says. She looks up at John. "Goodbye. Won't you walk me to the car?" John gives me a look like "Please?"

"What am I, your boss? Say good night to the lady. I'll see you inside."

I smile at Judy again, then turn to follow the big lady and Ivan and Petra into the editing room. John comes in a minute later with a vague smile on his lips.

It only took a few minutes, but Janda has it all set up and is playing back our tapes simultaneously on two TV's. It works just fine.

Janda says to me, "Not bad. It's raw. It's real. And one of the things I like the most is, it's very clearly trying to effect some change. We're into that here."

She pauses, looking at the screen some more. Then she swivels in her chair and looks back at me.

"Let me show you something," she says. In a deliberate way, she clicks a switch and stunning new images begin to appear on just one screen, almost like abstract cartoons. Surfaces move like pure mathematics, deep cones and spires. Material flings material into orbit and out again until it forms silky planes. A deep, spatial music surrounds me. It's all so abstract I don't have any idea what it means, something like wobbly disassembles of the universe— Roger Rabbit meets Albert Einstein, I don't know. But I feel like I've seen it before in my fun-house theater.

I look at Petra whose eyes are wide open. Ivan is impressed too. A silky woman's voice begins to speak, more like singing, actually.

"CREEE…"The sound hangs in the air, just an abstract syllable, but haunting like a chant. The screen image takes us smoothly, going into what could be a bottomless black hole of space.

"CREEAY…," sings the voice, now joined by two beautiful harmonics. "T-T-T-T-T-T-T" whispers a fourth voice in a rhythmic staccato. "CREAY…" the first voices sing again. And again…

"T-T-T-T-T-T-T"

"Create," I say aloud. The word has suddenly become clear.

The images change into drawings, animations of geysers, fountains of raw beginning, then hints of a pencil drawing, lines and circles, faces, shapes like cubes, triangles, pyramids, three-dimensional solids. Da Vinci drawings appear, Buckminster Fuller geodesic domes, elegant suggestions of all the power man has to begin things from nothing and bring them into a solid world.

"A creation is the raw beginning of something new. It's up to you, so DO IT!"

The tape comes gently to a stop, and our beautiful host looks at me again. I realize it's her recorded voice I've been hearing. She speaks at me in almost the same voice very hypnotic. She's done our show very well. I'm amazed at the parallel styles.

"We must create as best we can. It is our means of survival. We must have new ideas, have the vision to break the mold."

Ivan and I look at each other. For me, this is Deja vu to stuff I've thought all my life.

"Maybe we can help, be providers," I say. "That's what we were trying to do tonight ourselves." She is coming on very strong, pressing me back in my chair. Even though we were on course with this same idea tonight, I feel like she got there first.

For no good reason, my memory of our performance is of gawky kids. "It is important to be a mover," she says.

"Sure, we want to be movers, too," I say. "What's going on here?" I'm trying to avoid getting too sucked in, too intimidated.

John is looking back and forth from her to me. "A mover," he says, impressed at the idea. I look at him. I can barely read what's going through his head. It could be he's scared to death; I can't even tell. I think the guy cannot believe how far he's come since I found him.

Petra is quite impressed, and not intimidated. Same with Ivan. I think they like the sound of this a lot.

I almost forgot. I reach into my bag and pull out one of the remaining wands.

I hand it to Janda.

"What is this?" she asks.

"It's a premium item from Wand Enterprises. We gave them away tonight as a sign-up incentive. I think it's got potential to move people into action, get them to at least play with the idea that they can do things, and change things. We're inviting ideas, submissions."

She studies it like she might want to buy 25,000. Or she might laugh.

"You've got a strong presentation there," I say. "This must be the season for video experiments. What are you going to do with your piece? Can I expect to see it after the news one night?"

"We will begin to make our presentations soon, very soon. As you see, we are not quite finished. We are beginning to collect people together. Like you, I believe, we also are…recruiting."

Recruiting. I hadn't thought of us that way, mostly because I only have a vague idea what comes next. I'd just like to get people together, promote new ideas and understanding, like that.

She probably won't tell me what she's going to do. "What are you going to do?" I ask anyway.

She doesn't answer me directly. She pauses for a second, then pushes an intercom button and speaks into a microphone.

"Could I have the performance please?"

After a moment in which I don't know what to think, a group of people come into the room, all wearing surgical masks. They look a bit like doctors, perhaps at the delivery of babies, or madmen from dusty garages. It's an eerie scene, challenging my notion of the norm. I have absolutely no idea what's going on here.

One man takes his mask off. He's a bit of a wild man, red curly hair. Very handsome and intense.

"I have an idea," he says. "Look!"

He puts his hand on the large pad of paper he's carrying and flips back the cover sheet.

"I'm proposing we take the oil platforms that are not in production anymore and turn them into communities at sea. If we do this, we will create a vantage point above the sea, an ocean-sensing spot ideal for a broadcast TV station that can bring land-bound man back closer to our first home. I'm already in negotiations with Modern Oil concerning one of their platforms to advance this idea."

I look at Petra, thinking this vague notion might make sense to her. She's absolutely enthralled, sitting forward in her chair with lips parted slightly.

We're both distracted as a Black man takes off his mask.

"I want to test people for their aptitudes, a free test to identify talents. Then I will employ the people in fields of their talents for a period after the test, each person in a relevant apprenticeship program of my design. We will develop and sell on our own behalf any products or services we may create during this time."

That's pure idealism. Hopeless idealism. I thought I was an optimist. It sounds good though. These guys are certainly in the spirit of the cartoonist.

A tall, thin man stands, steps forward from the remaining ranks and pushes back his thick long hair: brown and grey. He takes off his mask and says, "I want to find artists to deal with our trash, assembling any collection they wish into any shape that has more value after they're done. We will see statues, elemental shapes, buildings, barricades. Treat the stuff like a raw material, experiment with it in any way. New uses will emerge to turn trash into financial gold, I know."

That one makes me think of Simon Rodia's towers themselves. I can relate to that idea.

A woman takes off her mask, steps up. I think she's with the man of trash, the way she stands with him, but maybe not. I always try to pair up women.

"Imagine," she says, "a gigantic balloon of marvelous shape and color that is covered with hopeful words from every tongue. As it travels from city to city around the world, people drawn to it will gather in its shade. Translators will explain the words, and baskets suspended beneath will carry greetings from everyone who has already seen it. Simple messages of unity. I am seeking corporate sponsors now."

Wow. That's a dream left over from some other era.

The last man to unmask turns out to be a strong Japanese man in a T-shirt. He looks like he's had a hard day of work. The shirt is dirty. I sniff the air. But his voice is clear and alluring.

"I see a large group of people, with circular mirrors in their hands, each catching the sun. The reflected beams of light overlap on a chosen target which bursts into flame, sparked by the collective action, a symbol of their focused energy."

This is getting to be amazing. I'm very surprised to see a group doing just what I had set out to do. And I gather this powerful woman is their inspiration, apparently. Or is that so? I ask her and she answers in a regal way.

"Here you see the beginning of our team, which is not unlike your own. We have nothing to lose by allying ourselves. Our ideas do not compete. We have everything to gain in our mutual support. We share the energy of innovation. We have decided to gather here at this station other such challenging ideas and their creators, to encourage them, organize them."

I can't help but wonder what Hugo would say if he could see her and know of this place. I'll have to take the time to check that out.

She is very striking, Janda, with her elbow on the swivel chair, looking at me. All four new men and the woman have sat down, and the room is quiet for a moment. But it's crowded. There are 10 of us in here, spread around in chairs before the wall of TV's and players.

"What are your names?" I ask.

The man with the long hair speaks: "Tony Amboy, physics, MIT. I live here now in Beverly Glen."

"Chris Walkman," I say. I would have guessed he'd be in a rock band. "I play guitar, too," he says.

"What are you doing with the trash idea right now? That's pretty unusual. Any progress yet?"

"So far, we've got a lot happening with glass as an additive to road surfaces. That's a pretty common idea that was going on before too. We're encouraging that and a lot of other recycling—disposable diapers into plastic wood and so on. I have a small consulting company that is driving this forward, but it's barely breaking even. Got a ways to go. I'm looking for artists who will settle for working in such a weird medium as trash. Meanwhile, I work in bands at night!"

I like this guy a lot.

I look at the Black man, talent-tester to ask the question.

"Jim Johnson," he says, "rector at the Church of Normandy. I ran a school in St. Louis for a while; it's still going. Also, I work a lot with social agencies. They do a lot of testing, too. But they don't normally try so hard to get people right into a work based on the findings. Motivation is a key factor of course. Guy's gotta want to work. So I try to get a lot of that in the program, too. I can be pretty inspirational if I want to. Janda here is about to help me broaden this kind of idea. This station is going to be a powerful platform, I think, and we could get a lot of testing and working centers going if we spread the word."

The way he looks at me he doesn't have to say anything else. These people are committed and it's clear why they are at the station. I really will have to check in with my Hugo. This is an impressive find, though it's still not clear to me what they are actually doing.

I almost have my mouth open to speak again when the oriental man stands up, unusually tall with piercing eyes and a very calm center. He feels like the leader in the room, along with Janda.

"Kenji Komo," he says. "I like your tape, Mr. Chris. We were watching it in the other room. You understand about power in the people.

"The reflecting disks I mentioned. I have 17,000 in my truck. When we focus the attention of so many people on one target, the target will notice, even if our people are spread throughout the city. How can we be caught? At the appointed hour we will direct our flame, then disappear! I come from Japan. My father was a warrior for the Emperor. Now I am one for Janda."

Kenji sits down, still looking at me. Janda shifts in her chair, and it occurs to me she might be wishing Kenji hadn't said those words just that way. The very strong note makes me uneasy. There's maybe another side to this group. Petra, Ivan and John are silent, but the mood has changed.

"What target are you thinking of, Mr. Komo?" I ask.

Janda interrupts: "He is speaking metaphorically, I believe, in that we may wish to draw attention to problems that creative thinking can address."

I think it is time to listen more, and learn.

The red-haired man of the fishing platform idea raises his hand.

"Don't be concerned about Kenji. He is our warrior it's true. But he is not a criminal. Nor are we. It is merely true that strong measures may be needed if we are to change the world. The world may be willing to change, but not able. We must help with good ideas, and...encouragement."

This is not entirely reassuring either.

"How will your ocean platform change the world?" I ask.

"I cannot tell you everything," he says, "but I can say it will be a place to love the ocean."

"Isn't that called Scripps Institution in La Jolla, California? Or the Woods Hole Laboratory in Massachusetts? What's Jacques Cousteau been doing for 30 years?"

"But Ocean Place, as I call it, will also be a symbol of what all the existing oil platforms could be. Rather than deadly mosquitoes sucking oil from the world and injecting poisons into the atmosphere, these platforms—since they are there now—can be eyes and ears and tasting tongues into the watery world."

"I think we still need oil," I say. "What's your name, anyway," I say.

"Jeff Down," says the ocean dreamer. "Sure, we need oil," he continues," like an addict needs drugs. Can you even imagine us without it? I don't think you can. Really, how bad would it be? Not fouling the air; not building a planetary greenhouse to burn us up, or drown us under the water from melted ice caps. We are a creative race. We must find other ways to chill our food, to move it to market, to move ourselves, to warm and light our houses. We must!"

His emotions are showing. "How will you get the platform?"

"As I said in my presentation, I'm talking with the developer right now—Modern Oil. I feel they soon will agree to my terms."

"Why?"

"Because the idea is right! We must make amends with nature, and make the platform itself a place of nature, a natural island. It must not be a knife in a wound, drawing earth's blood." His voice is rising. This guy is starting to sound as crazy as Kenji.

Janda starts to speak, to calm things down, but Petra jumps in, to my dismay this time.

"I agree!" she says. "My father's fishing grounds in Nova Scotia have almost been ruined by oil. Get those drillers and tankers out of the ocean!"

"I'm glad you agree," says Jeff. I'm amazed she spoke at all. "Modern Oil will see the way. Besides, Kenji and I have ideas to motivate them."

From crazy to sinister.

"Jesus Christ!" I shout. "You've got good ideas. Why do I feel this hatred? Like you're planning an attack? I cannot believe a group with your fine ideas would consider force of any sort."

Janda now has a chance to speak, and she is calming again, a Mother Superior.

"Force is something we will adopt with only the greatest reluctance, Mr. Walkman. Do not be concerned." There is a calmness in her voice.

"I will say this. We will present our good ideas—and thank you for acknowledging them as such. Karin Stoney here, who has not spoken of her Dream Balloon as we are calling it, will help draw new ideas to us. Then we will nurture them with the support of an interested constituency—one that I know is growing.

Here at KWIL, we have the means to identify and contact the people who are interested in change. In fact, that process has begun. Our goal is to inspire creativity, then to move good ideas into being, to improve the lot of all the people, to save our planet."

My anger is subsiding. This sounds very reasonable, and very powerful. How can I complain? Our mission is the same. She is right on my wavelength. But…my doubt lingers, I cannot say why. She holds so much in reserve. I cannot see through her eyes."

I turn to Petra, and John, and Ivan. "Shall we join them?"

Petra has fire and commitment in her eyes. Janda has touched her deeply. "Chris, the ideas here, and the commitment, is enormous. The exposure of the TV station lends great power to their noble ideas. I think we should join our forces, and our ideas." They've got a formidable supporter.

"Ivan?"

"I still reserve all rights to my projection system, excepting those you now have, Chris. But I feel good about this meeting here. I agree with Petra. Let us join our Wands to their voice, and their purpose."

"And John? I understand if this is more than you bargained for."

"Look, Chris. I've come a ways in a short time, thanks to you. As a salesman, I know well the power of TV. Let's take this and be happy with the coverage. We could sure get some s out there at least. There's 14 million people in the reach of this station in Southern California."

I turn slowly back to Janda, encouraged somewhat by their reaction. "You've heard the vote. I won't contradict it. Though there is still much to discuss with you, for now I tentatively agree we will join Wand Enterprises with KWIL-TV. Actually, I believe there is not much you can do here without losing your station's license. Have you covered that?"

"Our lawyers are on guard. We have our plan in motion. We will educate and motivate in the public view in ways that are effective. And we will make a difference."

That sinister tone peeks in like a shadow.

"Janda," I say. "You make me nervous. I want you to understand that."

"Chris," she replies, "like you, we intend to change the world. That should make anybody nervous. We will not flinch in our resolve." Again, she is deep and serene, and very intense.

After a pause, I say, "There is one other vote I must secure. On my recommendation, I believe I will get it. With that vote I will bring sponsorship. We shall talk tomorrow. Until then, we will not show our meeting of this evening. We will coordinate our actions."

It's been a very full day. I turn to my team, almost wondering if it still is one. "Shall we go?" We do.

SIX

A WAND IS BEING polished by delicate hands using a white cloth. They belong to a humble craftswoman in a small Mexican village. The wand is beautiful, made of fine metal with magical carvings.

Outside the studio window, gentle rolling hills are covered with yellow grass. A goat is grazing. The woman's dark hair falls over her cheek as she works serenely over the metal. She brushes the raven strands back.

Now she is done with this wand, so she places it on the top of many others in a small cardboard box that just fits perhaps 100.

The woman of the hills with black hair and lovely face picks up the box and holds it carefully before her in her lap. She bows her head as if in prayer. Then she stands up and walks from the room into the dusty sunlight. She approaches a man who is sitting with their son on a bench beside their house. A chicken pecks the dust. They are not poor. They lead a simple peasant life.

The man opens the door of an old Ford Falcon that is battered and rusty. The woman gets in holding the box; her son climbs in beside her. They drive along a dusty road into the village, to the hovel of a village mystic. He is an old, wrinkled man who smiles kindly at the family. Strings of teeth and feathers are tangled around his neck and hang down his chest.

The man takes the box from the solemn girl, places it carefully on an flat, circular rock and closes his hands in meditation for a moment.

From the wooden table before him he takes a shell, reaches in with fingertips of one hand and pulls them out dripping with clear water. Solemnly, with his eyes closed, he sprinkles the water on the wands, muttering incantations. The girl and her husband bow their heads.

The family gets back in the car. The box is placed on the front seat with them. The father drives through the mountains, down to a dusty border town where at the marketplace they sell the wands to a man who gives them pesos. Father smiles and hugs his small children and his wife. The box goes into the back of a pickup truck, which drives away.

The wands go into the box on Broadway, downtown L.A. The sign, "magic wand," now has a glow to it and I am resplendent in white as I pick up a wand from the stand. As I wave it in the air, sparkles trail faintly behind.

Before me is a dirty ragamuffin boy with his mother. I touch him with the wand and he's dressed in perfect overalls, his mother in a fine flowing skirt.

On a faded street corner is a bum with a bottle. With a wave he's in a fresh painter's suit, finishing the exterior of the building.

I look down the street and wave at the traffic. The crowded avenue becomes a beautiful lane with shoppers strolling amid trees, an exotic trolley system, overhead walkways, and vegetation hanging from the buildings, a moving sidewalk, everyone dressed immaculately. I smile a big smile and look at the wand. I put it in my pocket with great satisfaction and walk off into a waiting crowd of admirers: John, and Petra and Ivan. Even Janda is there. We all turn and walk down the street, pointing at the buildings, and I am very proud.

I realize that dawn has entered my apartment. I turn over on my back and stare at the ceiling. Wouldn't it be nice if things were that easy? But that's the power I feel sometimes. Or the hope.

One of the pens is on a stand by my bed. I pick it up and look at it. How could anybody get attached to this thing? Maybe it's just handsome enough for me. Or it's got just enough reference to an idea of drawing out strengths within.

My apartment is full of light—early-morning sun filtered through the plants out front. The deep bushes are projected as two-dimensional painting on the wall in bright sunlight and leaf shadows. It shimmers as the leaves jostle in the morning breeze.

As I feared, the elation of last night is now something else. I feel a bit like a two-dimensional projection right now. The rush to get ready for last night is over, and we're into a history tied up in something new—the TV station people. It seems perfect in some ways. I wish I were really excited.

"John, time to go," I say. He stirs on the couch.

"Good." He sits up, then stands up, takes one of my shirts on a chair and puts it on. He lifts my pants off the back of the couch, pulls them on. Not a bad fit, either item.

Now he speaks. "Chris, you know I've got questions. What do you say you answer some of them today?"

"Try me, John. I enjoy saying no." Can you tell I'm hung over from an overdose of self-importance?

"Chris, where does your money come from? Who's this sponsor you're going to talk to?"

He's asked this before but for some reason, after last night I'm more inclined to discuss it. Might be a good idea in fact. The way he phrased it makes it all seem very curious. And damn if it isn't. I mean, I guess it was a contest or something. Right? But really, I don't have any idea who Hugo is. What the hell could I even say to John? Which is a very good reason for not discussing it. I don't enjoy looking like an idiot.

I've been thinking about Hugo a lot. I want to tell him about the station and everything, as if it's mine. I know it's not, and I'm only partly sure I even want to be associated with it. Janda seems to have a lot of power there, but they also have such a different feeling, a readiness to attack or something. I'm not the militant type.

Still, they can mean a lot more money, if I can believe Hugo is serious about supporting good progress. I've concluded he's basically an eccentric philanthropist with a real eye for talent, that's all. That's what makes sense to me.

I finally come back into focus in my room, and on John's question.

"John, we're a team," I say. "You know how important that is to me. But I'm not ready to share everything yet. You know—and Ivan and Petra know, too—I can get us what we need, as long as it's a reasonable expense." I hope I sound convincing.

He's sitting on the end of the couch now, tapping his fingers on his leg in a nervous little way. Then he turns his head to look directly at me.

"You know, Chris, I don't mean to insult you, or attack you, but I've got to say this. I don't think anybody really trusts you yet. Not really."

This is a bit shocking to me, because John has not said anything so direct to me ever before. But I appreciate honesty.

"So…?"

"I mean, I certainly don't think Ivan and Petra do." He summons up some more strength.

"…And even me to a certain extent. I mean, sure we're all happy to take your money. And the people who signed up last night, they were impressed with your ideas, with the show and everything. We all loved doing it, and it said so much to people. But just because they signed a contract and took the wands…I mean, why should that guarantee any real cooperation in the long run?"

He pauses for a moment, takes a breath.

"I guess what I'm saying is I don't think we've really got any momentum yet.

Sure, we want to change the world. But we only got hold of a very small part last night. You think about the leverage Janda's got, it's enormous. And that's not even anything compared to the whole world. Where do our ideas start to kick in and really do some good, do you think?"

I look at him very closely. He's so different from the guy who pulled a knife on me. It's like you break open an ugly geode and there's beautiful crystals inside. I wonder if I made a lucky pick, or could anybody down on that Nickle turn around like this?

"I really appreciate your honesty, John. I'm not worried yet."

I wish either of those statements was actually true. He's got some good points. If I'm going to be a good leader, I better start thinking ahead better. A little more courage would help, too. But inside, I do have faith in the invitation we made to people to trust their ideas, and think about what they'd improve if they could.

I switch on the TV and pick up one of our leftover wrapped wands from the top of the set as a picture forms. I wave the magic stick at John, looking at him with one eye.

"I believe we will get our cooperation, and you are part of the reason." He smiles a big smile. "Judy looked great I thought," I say. I think it's fun that his dream is coming true. Almost did come true, if I had let him go to her place.

"…at the Hollywood Bowl this morning for a special sunrise service," says the TV. I look, and check. Its Channel 8 all right, KWIL. I wonder what the activists are doing."

"…a celebration of the days of summer when the sun, our father and mother, reaches its highest point above the horizon. Today, as we celebrate the earth and its place in eternal truth, our spirits, too, reach their highest point of understanding."

A man is talking at a podium. Words on the screen say the audience numbers 17,040, capacity at the Bowl. Every single person is holding a large disk of some sort. Some kind of a religious ceremony, it seems. The people look very eager, and happy and devoted to the speaker.

The camera slowly zooms over the heads of the crowd, in towards the man who is still droning on.

"…reminding us that nowhere in the universe has the unknown spirit yet found a more potent expression of His hope for the future than here on earth. And nowhere yet has that spirit more potently realized His purpose than with us here today."

The camera is almost full in on the preacher before I realize its Kenji Komo, Janda's self-described warrior from last night. Strange that no one mentioned this event to us.

"…So as the sun rises above the distant hill, let us be the receivers of its power, and the transmitters of power as well!"

The camera follows Kenji's hand from its gesture, across the hills to the near horizon where the sun is indeed just rising over the hill. I check my watch—7:25.

In a new TV angle of the crowd, it's clear that everyone is holding a circular mirror, just as Kenji had described last night. These look about two feet in diameter. The people in the audience are all raising the disks to their eyes, so they can look through a small hole in the center, perhaps an aiming device. It's almost comical to see the faces disappear behind this field of glass or metal or whatever it is.

"Thank you all for coming, and congratulations on the moment we will share."

The sunlight is now flooding across the crowd. I'm suddenly aware that a choir is singing higher and higher. On our screen, the shots of all these people are blended with a circular logo, like one of the disks, with an O in the center. This logo is perched on the top of the proscenium arch—and hitting across it are thousands of circular points of light, each from a mirror being aimed.

How strange. It's probably hard for any one person to distinguish the reflection they control. Each must simply share the knowledge that one will add to the others as they aim the mirror. The aiming device is fairly critical, I suppose.

The circles of light begin to settle in on their target—the circular icon—though many still dance around it.

As seen from the front, the audience is now almost invisible. All the people are hidden behind a sea of mirrors in which the camera catches only blue sky or green tree, occasionally a flash of the rising sun. But clearly, the focused rays of the sun are adding to the others at the icon, each reflection adding, I don't know, maybe a half a watt of sunlight to the total.

"John, can you believe this?" He shakes his head, fascinated.

"Concentrate on holding your aim," Kenji says through the microphone. "We are a single unit, only if steadfast in our united purpose."

The reflected disks of sunlight seem to respond to his words, converging in a tighter circle of now brilliant light. In a close-up, the target seems to be a circle of white metal. The choir is now itself at a new height of frenzy.

Suddenly, the metal sphere at the center of the icon explodes in the heat. It must be magnesium or something to burn like that. The flare is very impressive, even in the morning sun. It seems to sear the camera's sensors.

"It is done," says Kenji. "With this gesture we join in the cause of world celebration and betterment. We will unite our energy in the cause of universal salvation. If you feel as we do"—he's addressing the camera—"then call this number now to pledge your commitment. Join us in a new day on the earth. Call us, and join us. We need the strength of your own light."

A telephone number appears on the screen.

'Thank you for being with us, and we'll be right back for more reflections on the new spirituality of hope and personal power. Thank you for your generosity, which helps so much in making the world a place we can be proud of."

Kenji is much more of a salesman than I gave him credit for. Now, on comes the commercial for creativity that a showed last night. It still looks great.

"Jesus," John mutters.

"No," I say. "Not Jesus. This is new."

I don't get how I can be so intimidated by the force of these people, and in love with it at the same time. What an army Kenji's got. Once again, my own—our own—efforts at organizing and inspiring seem a bit feeble.

I look at our box of names, about 200 or 300 from the night before. In fact, there is very little difference between what I just saw, and what we did in Watts and Westwood. Both were religious ceremonies in their way. But Kenji's demonstration of power is impressive. Getting that many people out on a Sunday morning to come to this ceremony is quite a feat by itself. I guess it's clear from the message and the fun of it all how Kenji did it.

I'm suddenly very interested in having some assistance. I just don't feel up to the task of leadership on my own.

"John, what do you say we get together with Ivan and Petra? I'd like to continue our talk of last evening. And maybe this would be a good time to introduce you all to my sponsor. I think it's time to answer some of your questions, John."

I've still got the rented van full of equipment. John and I drive along the Santa Monica Freeway which is empty on this Sunday morning. We pick up Petra and Ivan at Ivan's studio. The van fits us all, even with the equipment still in it. No time to unload.

It's comforting right away to have our team back together. It makes me feel just a little bit larger against the world. I wish I knew it better. I wish I felt connected to them better. How does a leader do that, anyway?

I treat everyone to a quick breakfast at Gorky's downtown, to honor Ivan again for his good work. Then we drive to Bunker Hill, to the glass tower overlooking the financial district. Out front, the water drum sculpture is silent.

The elevator lifts us all up the side of the building. It's only been two weeks since I was there, what a larky day that was.

Then we're on the 31st floor, in the wide reception room again. For some reason, only now does it occur to me that I'm crazy to think anyone will even be there on a Sunday.

I lead everyone across the lobby, into the smaller room. It's empty except for the TV at the end of the grey table, which is turned off. Everyone knows we're about to meet this mythical sponsor I mentioned last night. I'm just praying that Hugo's around.

The blank TV is terrifying to me. I can barely bring myself to look at the screen.

"Turn it on, please," I say to Ivan. I'm a little shocked at my own voice. What the hell's the matter Mr. Hamlet? Catgut your tongue? Ha, ha, nonsense.

We stand looking at the TV. I hate it when I have to look to another source for support, to drive me. But hey, Hugo got me into this. I didn't ask for something to do.

The TV finally comes on. There's the room he was in, the back of his chair.

It's all empty—not a clue where he might be.

A voice from the set: "Jane, please bring me the file on the group we saw earlier, would you? Thanks."

A grey-jacketed elbow moves into the screen from the side for a moment.

Someone is sitting at the desk in TV there. Yahoo, I'm not alone.

"That should be a gentleman named Mr. Thomas Hugo. I'll introduce you if we can talk."

The sound of my voice attracts attention and Mr. Hugo's face pops into view on the screen. "Oh, sorry, hello, I didn't realize you were there. And good morning to you all. Who might this be?"

"Good morning Mr. Hugo sir. It's a pleasure to see you again. I'm very happy to introduce you to some of my compatriots that I referred to last time we spoke, about two weeks ago. This here is John whom I met down on skid row the afternoon I met you."

John nods a bit nervously, looks at me. What does this all mean?

"John, I'm happy to introduce you to Mr. Hugo who has been so kind as to make possible our recent good work in opening new channels of communication in the world.

"And, oh, I've been terribly rude…I'd like to introduce Petra from Nova Scotia who is very concerned about the health of our oceans. We are already beginning to discuss ways in which we can address that ENORMOUS problem of WORLDWIDE scope."

Petra looks at me like I'm crazy. "Hi," she says to the TV.

"And this is Ivan, our communications specialist, from Russia. He's very, very good and helped us PUNCH A HOLE right through the fence separating the upper class and underclass in our society, just last night. I believe—I should say WE believe—that we are poised to begin a very exciting new era in communications in which stresses and strains in our society will be relieved with a single puncture in the ideological and physical membranes isolating the parties…

"Everyone, Hugo is our backer. I can say no more at present about him. Unless, Hugo?"

"That's fine. Please tell me your name if you would. I don't quite recall?"

I'm stunned. "Chris! Chris Walkman?! You invested a fairly substantial sum of money in me and my ideas just two weeks ago, and following that I've taken some important steps to improve conditions in the world by…"

"Chris, can you describe any concrete successes you've had since that time that could be considered improvements to our collective lot on this frail planet?"

This is making me just a bit nervous. I look at the gang. I thought they might enjoy the humorous nature of this pleasant man, if he would just be pleasant at all.

"Concrete? Well, of course we're very pleased to have assembled a team of some 100 dedicated volunt…I should say dedicated, hardworking individuals ready to commit themselves to our noble cause. In fact, I have right here a list of perhaps 300 names we were able to collect at our kick-off event last night, every one of whom…"

"Chris, I'm impressed. How much money were you able to collect?"

"Ah…collect? Well, I'm very confident that the value of their ideas and commitment, if measured in dollars, would be…"

"Did you actually collect any money yet?"

John says, "I think we've got a really good team that will work very hard for $50 a day on the problems that face us."

"Chris—Mr. Walkman—am I to understand that you have now committed yourself to PAY 300 people $50 a day? What exactly would you have them do?"

"Well, sir, that's where the excitement comes in. I feel sure—in fact I know—that when all those people respond to our invitation, motivated as they were, that we will see some very powerful ideas emerge that can lead to outstanding results."

He looks up from writing something. "Quickly multiplying, I see that for you to gather together, motivate and hear the ideas of each of your volunteers on one occasion it would cost you $15,000, if you were to keep your bargain and pay them? Is that a fair assessment?"

"Yes sir."

"What else can you show for your labor?"

"We have a very exciting videotape that we can use again, perhaps to raise FUNDS for future endeavors."

I think I'm beginning to catch on.

"Very good. That's just what we like to see. Anything else? For my investment of, let me see"—he consults a list—"$20,000, I would expect to see at least one or two mountains moved by now."

"Sir, if I were to list one accomplishment that truly makes me proud, I think it would be helping John here to escape the degradation of homelessness, the crippling destruction of his self-esteem through booze and the pressures in our society to succeed. John, do you have any way to describe in concrete terms the value to you of our assistance?" indicating Mr. Hugo as well.

John says, "Mr. Hugo, I do not know who you are, or where you are. But I can say in all honesty, Chris is doing a great job. We've got a good team here, a team of the sort I thought I'd never join again. We've got a lot of confidence in him." What a liar. I appreciate that.

"Very good, John. Congratulations on your new life. And Mr. Walkman, I'm pleased to see you beginning to show some promise. It looks to me that one day you may be ready to move up to a new phase in our program, involving much larger sums of money deployed in entirely new ways."

Excellent. Now for my new pitch.

"Mr. Hugo, that is indeed gratifying to hear. I know all of us will feel very indebted to you indeed."

"Yes, that's right."

I press on, at a new height of excitement.

"One point I'd like to make is this: I'd like to convey or express what is at once a concern and an exciting new discovery."

I explain about our meeting with Janda and her team last night, about their really great ideas, some of them, and about my concerns for their militancy—about the meeting at the Hollywood Bowl this morning and the TV solicitation.

"It looks to me like this group is creating some sort of an army, Hugo. Frankly it makes me a little bit uncomfortable. Nonetheless, for now we are committed to help. We will be providers of ideas, of additional people to Janda and her team.

"Most important, if you agree, I am willing to lend them provisional sponsorship. Deferring to your sense of propriety, of course, I would recommend…something in the $200,000 range which I would be happy to release to them as their needs become clearer."

I'm really studying his face this time. He says nothing.

"My analysis of their operation is that they have the wherewithal to be very effective, especially if they get to a national level which they could do today if they wished. It's just a matter of them providing a product that stations will buy, or buying time themselves. With fundraising from a TV congregation, they could do that.

"Meantime, they have identified a series of projects that in my opinion are entirely worthy of funds, and if you agree, I will be quick to dispense them in an appropriate manner."

Hope. Hope. Hope.

"Chris, I think you are right to see excellent potential in this group. I am aware of them. Please use your judgment in how you support them. From what you say about Janda, I don't think you need to fear her power. I would say use it, my boy, use it.

"However, I see I need to clarify one point. Something that strikes me as very good about Janda and her team is this fact: that they have established very clearly their ability to raise funds from a congregation. That is something we always find impressive. Our financial ocean is large you understand, but it is not infinitely deep.

"As I listened to you talk just now, Chris, about your excellent program last night which may or may not have actually helped change the world, and about the good video commercials that might interest new people in your ideas, it's quite clear to me that you have talents similar to what we've seen in Janda and her people. Because of that, you have made me proud of you, and very happy."

He smiles an unctuous smile.

"Therefore, I believe we are truly ready to take an important step up to an exciting new level, one in which your obvious leadership and creative skills can be exploited to the fullest. I know your team will share your excitement, and mine, as I tell you: The sky's the limit as to what you can earn from your own congregation!"

He sits back in his chair in his TV room with the same beaming expression I remembered from the first time I saw him. And once again, I think he seems crazy.

"Mr. Hugo, I am terribly sorry, but I simply did not follow what you just said. Could you please repeat that? I am sorry to take your time up this way."

"Oh, Chris, you do too understand what I'm saying. You said it so eloquently yourself as you described the benefits you were able to bring to John. As I recall, you and he both felt pride that you were able to rescue him from dereliction and homelessness, restoring his self-esteem to its full and naturally strong state. You are right to consider that a triumph. Now it's time for you to do the very same thing yourself. It's time to cut those apron strings. You don't need to be embarrassed any longer about living off someone else's money. My boy, you can now move into the very tippy-top levels of self-sufficiency and of USEFULNESS TO THE WORLD by earning, from this day forward, every penny you need to make the world a better place, all on your own. The only way I know how to do that is to not give you another penny."

The shoe has finally dropped, right on my head.

"The other favor I'm willing to grant is that you plan to pay back the small, $20,000 investment we made in you, with reasonable interest according to this loan schedule we will provide, and I know you will want to do this.

"Of course, we have not forgotten about the little matter of the disability insurance scheme you've been involved in. I know you don't want to let that get in the way of a successful future, and I'm sure you won't. So, we'll see you one month from today with the first $2,000 installment. Meanwhile, get those good ideas of yours to work, and goodbye!"

As before, he suddenly shrinks to a blip and is gone.

This time I'm frantic. I immediately turn on the TV again. It warms up again, too slowly, and there's Miss Piggy, guest starring on "Sesame Street." No, no.

Where's the channel changer, the tuner dial? Nowhere. There's no way to change the channel? Nothing. I realize the TV has no tuner in it, that it's nothing more than a monitor. The cable coming from the wall is it. The set is totally remote controlled. I try the door into the next room. It's locked.

Oh! This is crazy. I came here for some kind of support, some sustenance against a challenger, and now I'm naked. I can't even look at these guys now. I'm helpless, a nobody again!

We all stand there in the dark room for a minute, lit only by the light from the hills and buildings outside.

This little team is so small. Even with the help of a backer, how could I have been thinking we could make some kind of a difference, against the ocean of people and habits and ingrained behaviors—against the odds? Now it's much worse than that. My position as leader is nothing. Here this guy gives me twenty-thousand bucks, makes me think I'm hot stuff, change-the-world kinda guy, a real hero. Then the rug gets pulled out. Worse than that, I've got three people thinking I'm some hot-shot leader with great ideas, a brilliant guy. Away that goes like a dream.

Ivan and Petra have wandered out of the TV room into the reception area and are sitting on the couch talking, but I can't hear about what.

John's still standing there, looking out the window. His left hand has absently reached out and he's drumming his fingertips on top of the TV.

I've got to say something quick.

John says, "Chris, look down there. On the street, there's a parade going by. It's the people from the Bow1 this morning. They've got all their stuff, their mirrors."

Great! Now my competition is parading right in front of me. It's weird they'd be down there.

Sure enough, several thousand people are walking down Hope Street and they do indeed have their mirrors in their hands. Bright circles of light flash across every building. I can't help but wonder where our warrior friend is taking his tribe next. It's a crazy sight. I hope they don't flash those things at me.

Oh, woe, maybe I do.

SEVEN

LOOKING OUT THE WINDOW at the parade of mirror bearers below, I'm waking from some dream, maybe my dream of changing things. I should never have answered that ad. Let's get out of here! John and I go in the other room where Ivan and Petra are looking out the window, too. I remember Petra's expression last night at Janda and her team. The heavenly look is back again.

"What do you think?" I say to the pair. Ivan has his arm around Petra and they're looking at me from a farther distance than they were before.

"It seems they have a mission," Ivan says. It sounds like, where's ours? "Let's go see what it is," I suggest.

We descend in the elevator not saying a thing. The tension is quite thick. We're standing on the sidewalk, looking south down the street after the parade. Mirrored dots of sunlight are still bouncing and dancing and streaking all over the buildings of the financial district. It's a magical sight.

I realize that if all the people focused their circle of light on one target, they might start a fire. I wonder if anyone realizes the potential of the crowd. Are there any police around? Aren't the people a menace? Aren't they disturbing the peace?

Goodness, I'm embarrassed that Hugo would do a turnaround on me like that. Hell if I'm going to pay him back his money. We worked very hard on that experiment, at his goddamn suggestion.

I almost feel I was tricked into doing something, into spending the money. He can't give it, then treat it like a loan. That's crap.

But damn it was nice to think about changing the world, as if it were a job. I still think we did something very impressive last night.

Ivan and Petra, still looking down the street, now turn to me.

I ask, "Don't you think we had a great night last night? I was so excited when those lights came on and we had a picture. That was a great team effort, team!"

Ivan says, "Chris, it was great. We were very happy to be part of it. But the one thing I want to know is this: What can we do next with it? Can we show it on TV? I don't think so." He sounds like "I doan ting so." I love the sound.

"Look, Ivan, I don't know what to say right now. You're right, the money's about gone. And yes, Mr. Hugo will not be available with any more funds in the near future."

Ivan scratches the side of his chin. "Are you going to do what he suggests, begin collecting money from people? We could maybe get people to pay for the Window project, or some other company to pay for it."

The idea of trying to raise that money from either our viewers or a company is exhausting to me. I can't even contemplate the effort.

"Ivan, I just don't know. I'm going back to KWIL to talk to Janda soon.

Maybe we can hook up with her team—NOT those crazies though." I wave down the street. "But, damn, I thought we'd see lots of money around there soon, if Mr. Hugo had signed on. Now it's going to be dry."

"Well, Chris, I will be very interested to see what happens net with you. But right now, Petra and I are very interested to know what happens next with the parade. So, you don't need to worry about us. We'll catch up with them and find what they are going to do. They seem to have such a clear agenda; we find that appealing."

He pauses for a second.

"Do you wish to come too?"

"I do not. It's not my style to join in mass groupings like that," though even as I say it, I realize that I'm full of air. What was I inviting people to do last night?

When I know, I'll really be getting somewhere.

"Ivan, you go, and Petra. And you, too, John?"

"Not I, sire," says John.

"Well, goodbye," says Ivan. "Goodbye," says Petra. "I'm sure we will talk to you very soon."

Some leader I am. Set me up with a commission, then take it away and I'm squished like a squashed banana.

Ivan and Petra set off down the pavement. He's got his hands in his pockets, still wearing the Dodger cap I saw him for the first time three weeks ago. Damn, why is it the finest creative people turn me on so much, yet I can't connect sometimes? I think my main challenge in life is to join up with people like that. What's it gonna take? One day maybe I'll know better.

And Petra is right by his side. I can just see her infatuated with him, a great agent. He's so strong and clear, with built-in drama. She's so protective. They're a wonderful combination.

I just look after them and the dots of light are still flickering on the buildings beyond them, somewhere near the black Modern Oil towers.

"Damn. John, is there any hope of saving this alliance? I can't believe something that got so hot the last few weeks just cooled off like that."

I'm looking at him. Has he got more insight like this morning?

"Don't worry about them, Chris. You worry about you. You brought us together, and made some great stuff happen. I would have said thanks to Hugo too, if he'd stuck around. But you're the one who came to Los Angeles Street and picked me up, got us all together. That's something, I think."

He pauses for a second, then says:

"I think we should try to do something to keep this going, even if we are going to run out of money. We're a team. Let's do something."

I can't imagine what. What happened to the energy? Does a little bit of money make that much difference? Or was it just because I went, "Hey, John: I've got confidence in you, here's some dough?"

I suddenly see those damn Reeboks of John's that caught my eye two weeks

"John, where did you get those shoes anyway?"

He looks down at the shoes, pulling his blue pants up at the thighs, lifting the hem clear. He looks up at me with a funny smile.

"I like 'em, too! It was simple, Chris. These shoes were laying in the street, in a bag. I think somebody put them on the roof of their car in the morning on their way to work and forgot 'em. The bag fell off right at my feet almost."

So much for my theory about latent enterprise in the guy. But still he surprises me.

"Chris, how much money have you got left? Exactly."

"We've got to take our rented TV equipment back tomorrow, and I'll owe some more money then. After that, about $1,000."

"You know, Chris," says John, "Let's take Hugo's idea, more or less. Let's call a meeting. I mean, that was our idea anyway, right, Chris, to get a bunch of people together and form a company, Wand Enterprises, and come up with new ideas? Let's keep it going."

He's absolutely right, we need to keep the basic plan going—to connect with ordinary people, inspire ideas.

John says, "Don't you want to find some real ideas? Let's call each one of our names from Westwood and Watts, then meet somewhere. I bet they'll come: it'll be $50 income to each, a planning session for the board of Wand Enterprises."

"John, we would need $5,000 to do that."

"Well, let's call 20 people. I'll be amazed if 100 people come anyway."

It's time to find a telephone, down the street at the Bonaventure Hotel, I presume.

John and I walk down the few blocks on Figueroa. Out front, limousines and cars are turning up like crazy for some big event. I ask the doorman what.

"Save the rain forests, a fundraiser. Robin Williams just went in. S'posed to be on TV."

Oh.

We head first for the cashier and change a hundred dollar bill. The fellow looks at me like I'm a vagrant. I guess I almost am today. I never did shave yet. At the phone bank behind the lobby we start our calls.

"Hello, Oscar Mendenhall? This is Chris Walkman. You met me at our big event on Saturday, out at UCLA. Yes, that's right, the Window event, the Watts and Westwood connection…I'm really glad you liked it…Well, we're taking step two today, gathering people together for a meeting of the Wand Enterprises shareholders. That's you. Can you make it today at 3 at USC? Yeah, we'll meet at the fountain, by the Bell Tower. Right, 50 dollars. Bring your thinking cap."

Typical. It takes about an hour to call our 20 sign-ups until we've got a list of yesses. Al the while I keep focusing on how ridiculously hopeless all this seems, to bring people to a meeting, throw away $1,000 bucks. What the hell is John going to live on when we get done? I'm not even sure how long I want him in my apartment, anyway.

The real question is what are we going to do with all these people? It's true, I've always thought a person was a basic package of energy. He can breathe, walk, talk, push and lift things and so on. Maybe we should set up a power plant with bicycles attached to generators. Everybody can pedal away like mad and generate electricity. Think of it: each person could easily keep a light bulb lit for several hours. Who's doing something more useful than that?

But look we've got a perfect chance, a group of randomly selected people coming together to do something to make the world a better place.

"So what are we going to do, Chris?" John asks.

"It's the basic idea of Wand Enterprises. We've got our wands, the desire to make things better. How can we do it? With new ideas, new energy applied to them. We've got to brainstorm, think, and look for new ideas. We're low people on the totem pole now, and new ideas are about all we can offer. Then, hey, at least we can take something back to the group at the TV station and join that crew maybe. Or find some way to make some money, get something going."

Do I really care? I'm surprised.

We get on the Harbor Freeway and drive down to USC. Why did I ever pick this place? I hate USC. It seemed midway between Watts and Westwood.

Suddenly it's very intimidating to see our 20 people arriving. John and I shake their hands, then leave them alone. Several are effusive about the Window last night, especially the ones who were in Westwood, I don't know why.

High concept, maybe.

"No, no plans for more just yet. We need your ideas for what comes next. It's all of us. All of us. We're gonna do it." And other empty ideas.

Someone points out that next to the fountain is a classroom, open with chairs.

We all file in, the people spread around in chairs, looking at me expectantly. My enthusiasm of just moments ago has suddenly vanished. How am I going to break through this barrier? Once again, here I am the leader, in front of a group that I've brought together. It's a fluke in fate, I got invited to change the world. Why am I at a crossroads? Tired, tongue tied. I can't talk.

John is beside me, he returns my favor and rescues me. He is talking. Take it John. I'm just listening. Save me, John, save me.

He stands up on the little stage in front of the classroom.

He's still the man of Jello, he moves slow, he talks slow. But now he seems even a little more brittle. I think he's tired, too. But for some reason he's taking on the show for now. He seems heavy now. Don't worry, if we fail we'll just go back where we were. Our only crime is we got our hopes up.

John looks over the small crowd again. He takes a deep breath. He says:

"Thank you all for coming here this Sunday afternoon. You know that after our event last night, there are a lot of things we care about. But, listen, I know you're really here because Chris or I offered you 50 bucks on the phone today. We promised we would pay you that, if we needed you. You will get the money today. The 20 of you here, that's $1,000. Chris will be paying you out of his own personal fund. Real money.

John must know that's not strictly true.

"You're right. I want you to feel guilty!" Laughter. "Do you know where that money comes from?" Silence. Show me. Move me.

"Do you care?"

"Hey, I care," says a tough guy I see through my haze. "And who the hell are you guys anyway? I saw you last night. My kid loves his 'magic.' But so what?"

He's asking just the question in my mind. But he's truly a jerk. "We're idiots just like you!" John says. Touche! "We think we can do something, I'm not even sure what."

"Look, I'm happy to take your 50 bucks for my trip here. But what do you really want me to do? And who's paying you? And why?"

"Good question, my man. You're right to ask. The fact is right now, nobody is paying us. For a while, we were funded. Now we are not. We thought we'd be able to pay you to make the world a better place. It works out that this is probably the one time we can do it, unless we get a pretty great idea here today."

John is walking around, stooped a bit more than necessary. The room smells of chalk dust. It's a small classroom, very bare with linoleum on the floor.

Supremely boring.

John starts again. "We all met with a man this morning, I don't know who it was. For a while we were part of something big, with some money behind it. Now we're not. Guess what? Like always, it comes down to us. We can look around for someone to lead, or pay, or tell us what to do, but that's really just wasting time. It comes down to us. To me. To you."

"What the hell are you talking about?" The jerk speaks.

"This is what I'm talking about," John insists. The 22 of us here—we can be something. You," and John points to a tall skinny black man. "What do you do?"

"I lay concrete driveways," he says, "when I get a chance." Him I like.

"So, you're a builder," John says.

"Sure."

"Then let's get you building things that matter. What really needs to be built in this city? In your town. Housing? Fix roads? Bridges? I ask you, what would you build if you had the choice?"

"Heck," he says. "First, I'd build a swimming pool at my house. But 'fore that, I'd need the money."

Everyone laughs.

"Not bad," John says. "You had a thought there. A swimming pool. An original vision of your own."

He sounds a little cynical.

"Now, can you take that one step farther and imagine building that swimming pool, really?"

The man says, after a pause, "No, I guess not really."

"Why not?"

"Because I'd never have the money. And I don't do swimming pools anyway." "Why not?"

"Because I do driveways, I said."

"Are you at the mercy of people who want you to make driveways? Or not make driveways."

"What?"

"Do you save to be asked to build a driveway?"

"Sure. I'm not going to do one unless I get paid."

"Look," John says, just a little exasperated, I mean have you ever thought about finding driveways—or sidewalks, or walls, or whatever, that need to be made, and then finding a way to get them made? Getting someone to pay you to make it because it should be done?"

"Are you crazy? Why should I do that?"

"Two reasons. One, you'd be doing something you think is worth doing, to make the world a better place. Two, don't you think you'd do it better because of that? I'm talking about individual action to the betterment of our planet.

"Remember the contract you signed?"

He puts his head up, looks around the room.

I say, "Why doesn't everyone get it out, their contract?"

The crowd reluctantly shifts into action. There's a shuffling of belongings as people reach for their little scrap of paper. We had them printed, the words I wrote in that little upstairs hotel room while John was in the shower. God, that's so stupid, I can't bear to have John bring it up. That all adds up to nothing right now!!

At least John believes in the thing a little.

"Anybody. Read it," John says.

A white girl, in front. She reads.

"Don't hurt people. Help them if you can.

"Respect their property, and yours."

John says, "Help 'em if you can. Simple idea. What if you helped everyone you could who needed a new cement driveway?"

"Fine! I like it," says the skinny man. "But who's going to pay me?" the man asks. "Or buy the concrete, or help mix it up, and smooth it? You askin' me to be all broke and a loner? I can't even do the thing at all without money! Why should I do it for someone who can't pay? Or won't? And if I do it for free, won't the guy I did it for expect it for nuthin' next time, too? Seems to me, if I do that, I've set him up to want even more next time, and made myself cheap in the process. I think that is horse doo doo. What's in it for me? I'll sell my driveways to the wanter, not the needer, and that's it."

Whew. This guy is real.

John is taken aback, I can tell. I can't help him because I still can't speak. But he surprises me again and jumps right back in.

"Listen guy. Just for the sake of talking about it, let's take 'making a living' out of the picture for a minute. However, let's leave in your 'quality work,' your skill, pride in what you do, and so on. In other words, how could we talk you into making a good sidewalk, one that needs to be there, without getting hung up on what you'll get paid, and who'll pay you? I mean, under what circumstances would you do that work for nothing?"

He doesn't say "none" as I expect. Why am I getting so cynical? He stares at the floor, stroking his chin in a thoughtful way.

"I can only think of a few," he says finally. "I'd sure do it for my family. And there I get love, and supper. For a good friend I'd do it. Even in those cases I'd need the money for the cement. Got to buy that stuff."

"Let's say I took care of the cost of all that, or say the stuff you needed just came there when the sidewalk was needed?"

"First, I'd still need money to live. I should get paid for my work, too, right?" He looks around at the others. But anyway, who's gonna say the sidewalk is needed? I still think right there, that is a tough call. What if two people say they need a sidewalk, who's gonna say who needs it most? We gonna vote? Man, there's gonna be an ar-gu-ment, and that's stupid. Really, they could probably both of them do without the damn thing anyway. I say, give me the guy who says the sidewalk should go there and he's going to buy it and put it there. That's the guy I want to build a sidewalk for. Please, make my life simple!"

He turns his head away, doesn't want to discuss that point any more. The guy makes sense—its basic supply and demand. I sure hope John knows where he's going with this talk. The original tough guy still hasn't got an answer about where we're coming from.

John says, "I thought you were that guy, the guy who was going to say where the sidewalk should go. You're the sidewalk expert."

The man says back, "I'm the expert at putting it there, not at saying where that *there* should be. Do you get it?"

I think John is getting caught. That sidewalk's gotta be paid for by somebody. If he thinks we're going to remake the world without paying for it, he's crazy. Hugo's money dried up, I can't do anything. And the guy's right, too; even saying what needs to be done, that's tough enough in itself.

An older man in the back says to John, "Listen Mr. Socrates, whaddya think you're gettin' at?"

The tough guy smiles at that. The old guy goes on, "Isn't good old capitalism enough for you anymore? The only countries in this world doing better than the U.S. of A are the ones doing capitalism better than us, like Hong Kong, and Japan and Korea. Karl Marx had his chance already with his damn communist system—from each according to his ability, to each according to his need, all that crap. If you noticed, that stuff is all kaput. Give it up."

John stares at the man, then looks at the floor, cupping his ear as if trying to keep it warm. Suddenly he sounds different.

"Look, my angle on the question is basically this. I just think there ought to be, that there needs to be, some god damned way to enfranchise the bottom folks in our vaunted capitalist society so they don't fall right out the damn cellar door and down into hell! Whaddya think anybody—is there any way?!" He looks around the room. "Well, is there? How can we take the two million people in this country along, the human zeros, and get them going somewhere? Everybody talks about the underclass like it's the coming of the living dead. Well, hell if it isn't.

"You wanna know what we're doing here today? I say it all boils down to that. How do we get the losers back on track? How do we make sure there's enough food to go around? How do we get people to get heads up? This country is really losing the battle on that." John is on fire.

"And listen, I don't ask the question only because people need help. It's not just that I'm some bleeding heart. These people—the losers, the poor, the homeless—they take, they drain it all out, they put nothing back. They are a drain on people who work. Plus they are a problem we all need to own up to. Can't we get something out? We have got to find some way to turn on a motor in the dead, so they come back to life.

"Look at me," he says. And everybody does, seeing a tall, thin frame, a plaid shirt, blue pants, his Reeboks. He's still a mess, though at least he took the time to shower and shave today. Shame on me for not.

"Two weeks ago, I was a bozo on skid row, drinking rotgut, sleeping in god damn doorways. Chris over here"—he points to me, and everybody looks—"this guy looks like a hero to me. He paid me some dough, took me in, got me lunch. He waved his magic over my head and said I could change my world. That guy lit a fire in me. I don't know why you did it, Chris! But that fire really got lit. It's in there, it's going again, for the first time almost since I can remember. And dammit, I want to change the world, and if there's one thing in particular I want to change, it's the waste of human flesh and spirit going on every day in this country.

"Can't anybody see the waste?!

"Can't we stop it? Can't we stop it?"

And all of a sudden he's crying. He is sitting down on the stage, in front of this group, which is absolutely silent, and very embarrassed. Goodness, things are really coming apart. Was that much bottled up inside him? He's changed so much, gotten so real so fast. It was just too much, but jeez he's moved this room. Everyone is stumped, especially me. He's hit my central point, too, and I hardly knew that's what it was. John has really hit it. It's the waste of human souls that's so horrible. I get it now—that comes before everything else.

I stand up. My legs are almost asleep and I can barely feel the ground. My head is full of cotton, wadded up paper, words from yesterday and today.

Everything's all gonna just crash down.

I walk over to John, put my hand on his shoulder just where he's sitting on the edge of the dias. There's no talking to him. I never did know what to do when a man cries. I did a few times, when my parents died. It just made me sadder. And now too.

But his pure emotion has helped clarify things, too.

He gets up finally and sits in a chair at the side, elbows on his knees, as if he's run a race. He looks at me a little sheepishly.

People are dying to get out of there, I can tell. In fact, one man in the back, the old man, does squeeze out. He catches my eye by mistake and waves a little wave. I can't believe he didn't even stay for payday. It's all very embarrassing. We're not quite the super showmen who put on the mega commercial last night.

John has hit the nerve in me so hard it's shocked me. There's no escape. But now is the time to talk and say something. Only a quiet voice will come.

"For me, at least, John makes it quite clear why we asked you here this afternoon. We want to save life on this planet. We want to ennoble all who are born and will die. We want to see that no one is hurt. We want to help them if we can.

"And we want to find respect for all that is theirs, and all that is ours.

"We can do so much to help the one who will not help himself. We can do it in so many ways. Today we have money to pay you for your trouble. Perhaps that will be a start. We will never have enough to do all the things that must be done.

"The question I cannot answer is this: How can we sustain the efforts that I can secure from you for only one day, with my paltry cash? That is the question, for without an answer the human waste will continue. Where, or what, is the system that can revive the spirits and power of all who despair? In return for the 50 dollars today I'll give you today, I ask that you think as hard as you have ever thought about this problem. Just think what we can do to bring back the souls who despair, or the kid in the ghetto who's lost himself to drugs. Let us think for a moment if there is any idea we have missed."

Everyone sits quietly counting the seconds until it's all over. But, hell if I'm going to let them get away easy now. I got my blood up almost.

"Many, many fine minds have worked on this problem, for eons. How can we save the lost who will not be saved? And I am not talking about religion, please. I am not some grubbing evangelist who seeks your money. I look only for an answer."

The silence is deafening. I'm afraid I sound like an evangelist myself, despite my efforts. Something is going to have to give here.

I finally face reality: "Perhaps, in fact, no answer can come from this small group. And there surely is not just one answer. We must at least be brave, and ask the question that does not get asked enough."

The men are fidgeting. Most look bored now, ready for big hopeless sighs, ready to watch a football game, anything else. I could use a good cartoon myself, about now. But like the singing frog, an ageless phenomenon has returned to haunt me.

A woman raises her hand and looks at me, very pretty.

"I know that proper education to build insight and self-esteem is what's needed, but maybe it just boils down to love? Do you think it could just be love we need?"

I'm almost startled by her voice. I'd expected these people to vanish into dust. "Love? That is a wonderful sentiment." I almost don't know what to say, the idea is so huge, all of Christianity and so on.

Finally, I find a way to speak: "I guess my question would be, is there anything we can do to foster it beyond what religion is doing. John here, and I, feel love for each other after only weeks, but it's not that simple. Fear is also a great motivator. And hunger. Self-preservation is a great motivator.

"You're right about education, I think that's extremely important, and has some practical aspects. I think that is really a key thing we should concentrate on."

I turn back to the 20. My eyes fix on a man in the front row, perhaps 40. His jaw looks set as if he grinds his teeth on one side.

"What's your name?"

"Reese, Paul Reese. I've recently moved from Hong Kong to the States. It's just not safe over there anymore, as you know."

He's got a slight English accent, or Australian.

"I don't want details about you," I say. "But please speak for a moment about what answers you see. Your vision of what we might do together as part of Wand Enterprises. What's the wand you would wave?"

I fish in my pocket for my wand, and hold it up as a reminder. It makes me smile because it's so silly.

He pauses for a moment, standing with his hands in his pocket, looking at his feet. Then speaks.

"I don't know who you are Chris. You're acting like you think you're some messiah. But I thought I'd take $50 for a trip downtown today, why not?

"Your show at UCLA the other night was funny. I don't disagree with you at all. The world is indeed in sad shape. But I can't imagine where you're going...bringing a bunch of no counts together to ask their ideas." He looks around as if to sneer.

"Paul...vision please!" I shout, but I'm beginning to realize how foolish my basic concept was—to think that just bringing minds together we'd think of any answer to the eternally insolvable problems of poverty and on and on.

"Aright," Reese says, "for my 50 bucks, here's vision. I think the lady's idea—and yours, your idea about education being the core— is right on. The reason for the waste is lack of understanding on the part of the wasted.

"The discussion between Mister Socrates and our Man of Cement got right to the main issue: nobody ever gets something for nothing, even if they need it. The fact that probably two million children starved to death this year around the world proves my point.

"You did something fundamentally right, however, in lifting John from the gutter. You gave him a job and told him that if he works, he'll get ahead. It's not important that he believes he must work. It's important that he DOES work."

It occurs to me that my assignment from Hugo had a similar effect on me.

"As you said quite rightly," Reese continues, "self-esteem and self-respect are at the center of it. The problem is, you can't legislate improvements on that score.

"Here's my idea, and it really was inspired by your TV show the other night, wasted as that show was in many respects: We need more of that, touching more people face to face that way. I think you can use that set-up to show people the world, say in the projects, or on skid row or asylums, wherever, to show off the number of opportunities outside. It will show people ways to escape, new roles to play.

"Sure, we all sit at home and watch television. We see the world. But you're not really engaged with it, or really dealing with the challenges of life. For the first time at UCLA, when those kids in Watts were jiving with those kids around UCLA, I got that feeling. People were really in contact with one another."

This is the best thing I've heard in days. I think this guy, Reese, is right on the wavelength we were on a week ago.

I ask, "So what do you propose?"

"That's it. Keep doing what you're doing. Keep putting people in direct contact across barriers. Maybe put a director in your Window setup to manage the interaction a little. Get some real learning in motion. Encourage people to really deal with one another in very different areas. Most important, take the system to where the people need it, down to John's hometown, maybe. Use it to confront the people who are stuck."

"Paul, now I do want to know what you do." "I'm a teacher."

Ah, it makes sense.

"Paul, we have one minor problem with the idea. It cost about $15,000 to do that experiment the other night. I agree with you. But we need a way to make that pay, or something."

"Use phone lines. Hell, maybe you just take people out to where you want them to see and be seen. Can you imagine taking some bums from skid row over to—well, here maybe. Wouldn't that have some impact?

"Sure. People could wear clothes pins on their noses?"

"Damn, Chris, whose side are you on? Are you open to ideas, or what?"

Another man stands up, well dressed, from India I think.

"Hello, my name is Indi Anduu. I have lived here in the United States for almost 10 years now, but I am from Bombay. I am a lawyer in contract law, and I teach here.

"Another point that I think was missed a moment ago, and Chris you may barely be aware what you've done. That is, you've introduced the idea of a contract into this business of volunteerism and individual development.

He continues: "I think the concept of contracts is so important that you and we should consider it further. I know some schools use them now to get the kids to focus on what they're doing. The child expresses in his own terms what he feels is important, with guidance, and then contracts with the school and with his parents to make some progress towards it.

Meanwhile the parents contract with the school that they will provide support and a place for the kid to do homework undisturbed and so on. It helps lock people onto a course they want to be on anyway, just like any good contract.

"I think you're doing that with your contract, to help people if you can, and so on. I know there's no way to enforce that. But again, each person who signed it knows they told someone in writing they would do that. To me, you're on the right track with that one."

I'm quite impressed with Mr. Indi's idea, because it makes good intuitive sense to me. Get a student or vagrant or criminal or whatever to define what they want, then sign them up to get it, with incentives or penalties for failures. The idea would be for people to commit to their own ideas as a worthy goal by itself. That's the basics of taking responsibility, I think.

Other ideas come in, but I'm completely wasting the $1,000, which is play money by now anyway. But I really do like the contract idea very much. That chimes a chord for me.

Someone else mentions very small business loans for homeless or the poor so they can buy a shoe-shine kit or a sewing machine to begin a business. Welfare, workfare, more education ideas, more contract ideas. Paul Reese has more to say on that, and goes on to propose much more activist television in pursuit of education for all. That too is an idea that appeals to me.

But when all is said—and a lot is said—I still feel quite helpless. One person, only—and this surprises me—only one person says we should do something like get into a political process more, maybe get an initiative on the upcoming ballot of more money for the poor, or something. Nothing happens there, no consensus.

The consensus is, I'm afraid, that without money you just can't do a damn thing, except through volunteer organizations, which seem so volatile and ineffective.

As we pack it in, I decide probably for $1,000 we should have taken out John's old skid row buddies for a drink and dinner. Ha ha. But everybody said they'd stay in touch and some even said they'd be willing to work without pay in the future. Great. I don't think that promise is worth a cent.

Anyway, the meeting comes to an inconclusive end after 6 o'clock. Everybody gets his or her $50 and I am not in for a good night's sleep, I can tell. I feel as helpless and impotent as I ever did. Twenty thousand bucks for zip. Ain't that the ultimate insult?

EIGHT

My bed is soft. I'm alone in my apartment for the first time in two weeks.

Lord let me stay here, please.

A glass of orange juice is on the end table, where, despite the Lemon Pledge, a coating of dust has settled. Some things need attending to.

At least there's no cat and no fleas. How Kitty got out of the apartment I'm not sure, but she's gone and that's a relief in some ways. The place was like a war zone; the cat was desperate. It would be funny, except I feel like a jerk about it. Two flea bombs killed the fleas even in the deep recesses of the carpet. The guy can't even take care of a cat. What's he doing trying to change the world?

"Who Framed Roger Rabbit" is playing on the VCR. Eddie the human detective has just gotten into his bed after a hard night investigating. It looks like Roger the toon has been framed for murder. Eddie plans to check it out in the morning. Except, here's Roger with baggy pants and long ears hiding in his bed. They scream! I love it. Wake up everybody, there's a toon in your bed!

It's great to be under the covers, looking at a movie. It must have been hard to make those toons look like they live in the real world. They had to make a stage five feet off the floor of the studio to operate the props that toons would hold later, once the animated characters were drawn in—guns, papers, whatever. It's very tough to bring cartoons into the real world, and it's the same for your imagination. Everybody wants to get into the McDonald's happy-world commercial instamatically and have a fast car and a beautiful babe with great hair. Good luck.

How about all those guys down on skid row where John was? They're down in the bottom of an energy well; how do they get out? There's John in my mind's eye, crying on the floor in that classroom. How do you rocket people out of that kind of despair? No way, but in my frustration I want to take homeless people and shake each one by the shoulders and shout, "WAKE UP, WAKE UP!"

I wonder how John's doing. After our discussion group, he couldn't talk, just like me at the start of it.

I look at the list of our participants. Who knows if we'll see 'em again? It's an interesting list, though. All those individuals and talents.

John only had one thing on his mind; he wanted to see Judy. He sort of croaked it out: "Chris, I want to see Judy tonight. She's expecting me. Will you take me there?"

Sure!

The van was parked out on Figueroa, which suddenly seemed like a very bad idea when we got back to it. But all the equipment was still in it. Goes back to the rental place tomorrow.

I drove John back over to West L.A. It felt like a Big Game was over and all the people were streaming back to their homes, going separate ways. My mind said something big was ending; all our energy was going back into fragments. I thought every car on the freeway held somebody who didn't give a damn about John or me, or our hopes and what we did Saturday night in Watts or Westwood. They seemed to say, "Tomorrow's Monday, I've got to get myself together." That was just me, projecting again. You can't tell what someone in another car is thinking. But Sunday nights always feel that way to me. You try to gather your energy again. My energy is usually gone after a weekend of trying to get some hopeless project in motion.

Anyway, we got off the Santa Monica Freeway at Overland. The sky was darkening, the clouds moving in for a closer look. It was about 6.

We drove up wide Overland to Pico. John had directions to a house on Mentor. It was a thin street, the house was small, rose-colored, with a large Bird of Paradise stuck in the dry dirt out front. Warm light was seeping out curtains in the bay window.

As we walked up to the door, a piano was playing, not badly, echoing in a room with hardwood floors. We knocked on the door and there was Judy. She didn't seem surprised to see us. John must have called her during the afternoon. I'm really glad he did. She looked so nice, a little bit overweight, probably at 50 or so, just a little bit older than John. I never asked his age either, but he's about 48, I'd say.

"Hello, gentlemen," she said, making a joke. "Will you come in?" John looked at me, his face empty, but then he smiled at her. It was a Hallmark moment. I agreed to come in for a second. She offered us both a nice glass of wine, the pink stuff—White Zinfandel.

We sat in her kitchen; I kept planning to go. I wanted to be alone, but we talked. She said again how much she liked our Window event, but where were Ivan and Petra? I said we'd probably see them again.

John and I described the meeting at USC with our 20 people. She was fascinated and told John he should have said something, she would have come. John said he wished he had, too, except that it was a rough meeting for him. He confessed to the crying. She was concerned to hear it and she touched his hand. For a lady fairly settled in a nice place, she was warm to this bum, seeing the same things in him I do now. Not that I did at first. The guy tried to kill me!

She offered us spaghetti. I wanted to be alone, but I stayed.

"What are you going to do next," she asked me again. "You're so ambitious in some of what you do."

That seemed like a good way to sum it up.

"Judy, I had a backer for a short while who offered me money to change the world and make it a better place. We did something that I hope was useful. We may find it will be useful in the future somehow. But right now, I'm not sure what we can do next. We got a good solid list of talents today. We got some good ideas. But I just don't think there's anything I can really do now. The money's gone."

I noticed her napkin rings had little angels around the rim. She's got nice taste. The fact that the money was gone hit me again. We had thrown away $1,000 in the afternoon. What was I thinking?

"I want to know what you'll do now, John," I asked him. "My apartment is not that big as you know. Are you going to go back to sales? Or something?" I was pretty obvious.

"Or something, Chris," he said. "The world is my day-old oyster. Pee-yew. I'm ready to try almost anything."

He sounded like a classic hippie, all of a sudden.

He continued. "Judy works at a bank on Pico, across from The Pizza Place. She said she would introduce me to her boss. And I may just walk up and down the street here to see what might open up. It seems like a comfortable neighborhood.

"And Chris," he paused, and looked at Judy as if to let her know that now was the time: "Judy has offered to let me stay here while I get settled."

They looked at each other as soon as he said it, as if to make sure they weren't making a mistake. I didn't think they were. The power of that is not to be underestimated.

"Her husband died two years ago," John continued, "of AIDS, so she's not crazy about living alone. She has decided to welcome me as a guest, and I will pay her rent when I can manage it."

Judy said, "Chris, this fine man is at serious risk of returning to his streets if we let him. I think you have done something wonderful for him so far. I thought it would be good for him to have a place to stay."

I wasn't sure how my apartment was going to feel after another few months of cramping our styles. Not that I have any style. But this was very good news.

So I left them there, an improbable but charming new family unit. I came home, the wine still warming my brain. I turned on the VCR.

The mail of the last few days is on the end table by my bed, where I dropped it. Roger Rabbit is over, I don't even know how it got to the end; it's just snow on the screen the tape at its end.

Hmm, didn't see this before, a letter from the State of California, probably my disability check.

A note inside:

"Dear Mr. Walkman:

"Your check was delayed because of questions that have arisen regarding your accident. Please report to the State Disability Office at your earliest convenience for review of your case."

I suddenly see Mr. Hugo's ruddy little fat face saying, "Not another penny," and "We have not forgotten your little insurance scheme." What the hell could he know about my accident? If he knows anything he probably knows enough. But why would this letter arrive now? He just told me today about the reminder. He can't be connected to this letter.

Maybe he's not, but the entire awfulness of that scene with Hugo comes back to me, amplified by the loss of my only other income. This is not news I would expect for a Sunday. Can't a guy get some charity? My relative euphoria of the evening is gone. Looks like my stupid little adventure has left me worse off than before.

My experiment in activism and altruism is turning into just more crap. Our Window project was a great idea, and I thought sure could do some good. There's all that tension between blacks and whites and so on. I just don't know why the Window didn't do something. We should be on our way to Nirvana by now.

Heck, I don't know, maybe when those ideas start coming in. But right now, not much new direction, no new empires of freedom, no new world of sleepy hopefulness.

And then I'm flying through the air, arms spread wide. The ocean glitters below me, now coastline, now a city, dry and dead. I alight on a street in a residential neighborhood where yellow grass grows through cracks in the road. Bushes and tall weeds are brown. Once well-watered, the neighborhood has tuned to desert. Where are the people?

Leaping skyward again, I climb as if up an airy slope. Cars are everywhere below, covered with dust, tires flat. The streets are almost indistinguishable from the surrounding earth. With man gone—my dream does not reveal why—his signs are disappearing, too. The desert that was here before is returning.

I realize dimly that I'm dreaming, and it's a sad dream of where we may end up. It looks very real on my internal screen. Our earthly perch is precarious.

I allow a vision to continue in my mind of a lone skyscraper, just one of the thousands that might one day be abandoned, to disintegrate slowly over centuries. Streaks of rust bleed down its sides. Dirt dims the windows. Stone facing drops away.

After hundreds of years, the steel girders are weakened. With the shaking of a small earthquake the building cracks and twists down to the earth with a dusty sigh like a tired old lady. No one is there; she makes little noise. But her guts spill out—desks well preserved, and filing cabinets with ancient, meaningless memos that blow away.

Over a million more years, the settling continues, the carcass rots, or perhaps is preserved under sifted sand. Who will ever know? Prosperous cockroaches, only.

Now the TV has come on because the tape has reached the end at last. The VCR's tuner switched over to the evening news. A man is talking about more gang murders.

"Also in the news today, activists literally put the heat on big oil in a downtown rally this afternoon that was finally broken up by police.

"Calling itself the Knights of the Sun, a group of religious demonstrators promoting solar power over gasoline, gathered in the downtown financial district after a morning service at the Hollywood Bowl.

"Their point was to tell big oil to look to the sun!

"But their warm greeting turned to trouble when they turned up the heat by turning reflecting mirrors on the headquarters of Modern Oil building at Figueroa and Sixth."

The picture now shows the crowd of Kenji's warriors on the sidewalk and gathered in the streets around the building, concentrating the sunlight at the sign on top.

"Though the protest was peaceful and orderly in all respects, police finally decided that the intentions had turned violent when they realized that the heat being generated from all the mirrors was actually causing damage to the sign, where the reflected sunlight was being concentrated. With loudspeakers and finally with runs through the crowd, police broke up the effort, arresting several of the leaders.

"Jean Jennings was one lady from the group who agreed to speak to us."

"This was not intended as an angry meeting, but rather as a ray of intelligence and hope directed at this company, a statement about people of power and the power of the sun, talking to a company that should have good sense to be developing this energy source more fully. It's time we stop our reliance on foreign oil, time we unite to live sensibly with the power of the sun, and the power of the people."

The newscaster continued: "Despite the non-violent intentions, the damage to the company sign was considerable."

It looks melted to me!

"Executives from Modern Oil who arrived on the scene said they intend to press charges of wanton destruction and vandalism. The city is also considering charges of unlawful assembly and creating a public nuisance. Three leaders of the group were out of jail on bond this evening but would not speak to our reporter."

The newscaster-anchorman turns to his partner, the pretty Varna Black, whom I watch every night on this news program.

"I'm embarrassed to say, Varna, that one of the people involved today was our own news director here at KWIL, Janda Evers, one of the ringleaders of the crowd this morning.

"It's a shame, Bob," Varna replies. "I can agree with some of their sentiments, and I know we were all moved by the ceremony this morning at the Hollywood Bowl. I like my sunshine. But it's tough to support the violence, even if it was an accident."

"The story even adds insult to injury, Varna, because the group was attacking the office building of this station's parent company, Modern Oil, using mirrors that quite possibly were purchased with money from Modern Oil.

"Yes, I would say this has put a cloud over the future of the Knights of the Sun, Bob.

"In other news this evening, a light plane carrying three people…"

I'm not surprised one bit. Not one bit. What a bunch of idiots. God damned idiots.

I jump up from my bed and walk around the room like a runner rounding the track.

"How could they be so stupid? Unlike this morning, I've got to admit I should have expected it. In retrospect, Janda and Kenji and Jeff the oil-platform man were quite clear about their violent intentions.

Actually, since when did I even care that much what they did? Maybe for a while, actually. Maybe it was intimidation, maybe fear at seeing how far I have to go to really cut loose. Janda and her team all seem so aggressive and sure of themselves. That's one fault I have never had. Confidence comes to me like a passing fancy. The 20,000 bucks went a long way to building my confidence, while it lasted. Then try one idea and I'm done. Cleaned my plate of the one idea I had.

My anger is subsiding, but the idea has entered by mind for the first time since last night—I've got to see Janda, I've got to get back to her and the group. That elemental something, that fire of doing something was great. And stupid as they were today to blow it, that fire, the directed energies of their people, was fine.

There's a paradox there; go, but don't go too far. Dare to fight, but don't fight too hard. I don't know where I am on the spectrum at the moment. Nowhere, I guess; in my cocoon with the TV on, doing nothing.

My hand goes on the phone. But no. But yes, butt head.

"Information? The TV station KWIL, please."

Calling the number; just the official "We're closed" message. Why am I trying to do all this crap on a Sunday? I call back to Information, to ask if there is a news department number for KWIL and can I get it?

"KWIL News." It's a suspicious young fellow. The newscast is into sports by now, and I can almost hear it in the background.

"Ah, hello. Is Janda there?" What is her last name? Janda Evers? "No, I'm sorry she is not." He stops, offering nothing.

"Look, I realize she may be in an awkward position there. How can I arrange to see her?"

"I'm sorry but I don't know. Perhaps call back tomorrow and ask for the station manager."

"Does she work there any more, after today?"

"I don't know," is the answer.

"Last question, your honor. Weren't you folks just a little bit open with your dirty laundry tonight? Your comments made everybody look a little sick, I thought."

No way am I winning points with this guy.

"Call back tomorrow please, I don't know anything more about Janda or the events of today. Thank you for calling and goodnight." Click.

One more question, now that you've hung up. What the hell is an oil company doing with a TV station, anyway? And how the hell did it manage to pay for 17,000 reflecting mirrors without knowing about it? This situation is crazy. Who can I call? I'm getting worked up now. She's going to have a lawyer. Maybe I can find the lawyer. The Times must have a reporter working on the story. Maybe they'll know.

And where, dammit—where's John's number when I need it. Judy gave it to me. Here.

"Hello Judy. Thank you again for the great spaghetti. I'm sorry to bother you; can I talk to John?"

Pause. It suddenly occurs to me I may be interrupting John at the high point of a dream. But no, she says "I'll get him; he's in the other room." Other room? Must be innocent.

"Hel-lo?" It's the ice cream man, talking slow. I forgot, too, that the wine may have been too much of a good thing. He didn't say much about it to me but it's possible the battle he fought with booze is not over, just because he's away from Main Street.

"John, hi, I'm very sorry to bother you. I wasn't thinking. Did I break up anything?"

"No Chris, I fell asleep in front of the TV."

"Did you see the news on KWIL?"

"No, Chris, Judy just woke me up."

I explained about the stupidity of Janda and her crew today, how they'd been arrested, apparently. But I could tell the ice man was melting, too spent to care.

"John, I'll call you in the morning. Sorry to bother."

What time is it anyway? 11:30 at night. I've got to find out more.

"Information? Can I have the number of the L.A. Times editorial department, please?"

"City Desk, Brandon." The voice is gruff and weary. Sounds like the beginning of a long graveyard shift.

"Hello. Is anyone there still working on the case of the crowd with the mirrors today? I just saw on the news that some of the people were arrested. I thought I might be able to help some, maybe add something."

"Hold one." No wasted words from whoever-it-is Brandon. Then a new voice comes on.

"Mosey."

"Hi, are you covering the story on the Modern Oil mirror attack?"

"I did cover it. Story's gone a while ago. What's up?"

"Were you there?"

"Yes, I was," the reporter says.

"Do you know who was arrested?"

"Yeah, a man name of..." He's looking at something. "Kenji Komo, the leader, and a couple of other people. My city editor said you had something to add? Did you know any of the people?"

"No. Yes. Not really."

"Look, I'm going home, two minutes from now. If you've got anything, I'm delighted to talk to you. Were you connected to this organization, the Knights of the Sun?"

"I watched them on TV this morning. I just thought it was amazingly stupid how their pitch this morning, which had some appeal to it, evaporated tonight. That's the end of the organization, right?"

"Could be," the reporter says. "And what's your name, by the way?"

"Chris Walkman."

"It's not clear to me if it's the end of the organization. Don't know where you've been, but they've been growing for some time, but until today not so obviously active against the oil companies. That broadcast was only one of many, and most were just about the sun. That mirror trick was new. But I do think that was almost all their people today at the Bowl, and less of 'em downtown. I'd say this is the first of what they'll do, not the last. They've got some steam up by now. And even as a group today, police had a hard time stopping them. They could spread out so much and be even harder to stop."

Suddenly, I'm in a mood to offer something. "I met Janda at the station the other night."

"Who's Janda?"

"She's the station's weekend news director. Didn't you know? She was arrested today, too, I thought."

"No, never heard of her. I must have missed it. But I'm looking here—nothing on the police report. No sign of her name that I see."

Now that's weird. Her own station mentioned tonight that she was involved, that she was the leader, and that the station's owner, M-Oil, had even paid for those mirrors. It was just on, 10 minutes ago."

He shouts off the phone, "Hey Brandon, this guy says she just saw on Channel 10 that their news director was involved in the mirror event today. They admitted it on the show. Can we re-plate and get that in for tomorrow?" I can't hear the response. Then Mosley comes back on the line.

"So, what else can you tell me? Did you know she was involved?"

"Yeah, I was over at the station just last night. She was."

But I stop. Why should I talk any more about this? The woman is becoming a total enigma to me, totally fascinating, and angry as I am, I really don't feel like making her situation worse. The action side of her I find so appealing—the doing, the anger, the purposefulness.

Mosley is prying now.

"Say what? You were there last night? What happened?" Cat's got my tongue again. I have a hard time talking.

"Yeah, I met her, I was showing her some footage from a project I was working on. She was interested, we talked about it. It just struck me that she was a motivated person, that's all, with some deep convictions.

I'm surprised I am saying this, like I'm discovering it for the first time. The creativity stuff I don't even mention, though it's really on my mind.

"I guess she just seemed, powerful. And I'm sorry if she went too far."

"Can you tell me what sort of convictions she held? It never was very clear to me what their group was after. I know they were all yelling today about stopping the drilling in the channel.

My fear of talking with this reporter gives way to the desire to do it.

"It was sort of complicated. She had a lot of people there, this guy Kenji who seemed like a real radical, somewhat dangerous almost. And there was another guy—Jeff somebody, I forget his last name now—who was also into fighting with M-Oil. About oil drilling platforms. He wanted to make them into a hotel or a viewing station—like a forest lookout. She seemed supportive of them. But she also had several other people who were suggesting really great ideas, like testing people to see what their aptitudes were and helping them focus on them. That seemed like a great idea."

I explain the others—the balloon lady; the trash sculptor. I had a feeling there might be others I didn't meet.

"She was forming a team and it had really one central idea… just create things. Find elemental ideas any way you can. That seemed good to me. I'm afraid it ends up looking like she was just encouraging chaos. That's what she got today."

"Did she seem to be encouraging Komo?"

"All she said to me was that sometimes people have to be encouraged to do the right thing."

Damn, I shouldn't have said that!

"Look, this is not an interview, right? I mean this is off the record? I didn't think she was into violence."

"Chris, I've got to go check out some details on your story now. But you've been a real help. Sounds like that lady made an impression on some people. I'd like to talk to her."

Me, too.

NINE

MAN. MAN OH MAN. Man o' war. Manna from heaven. Man-child in the promised.

Child I feel like—baby, lost, wondering, discovering afraid, needing. Hey, I've always been in need. But this seems new and different, something almost like passion. It's late and I'm tired. What a long day, couple of days it's been.

Rented Ford van, in the street, parked. How strange to own this cargo tonight, these wires and screens, speakers.

I find the keys in my pocket. The front seat of the van is cool. Smooth metal of the dashboard reflects the streetlights in a thin white line. There are the boxes, the dials, the switches, the speakers, the projectors. A wand/pen is up on the dash, in front of me. Is it one of the last ones? Can't be many left.

I look again at this child's toy, the black pen with words on the side, Magic Wand. This thing is now something more than it ever was. The Mexico dream comes back with its hopeful empowerment. Obviously, it is not only I who sees the power in these objects. Just look at the side and the words. Someone understood.

Imagine me, picking up a wand and changing the world? How sappy, fabulous, infantile. But what's the difference from all those years of church; they encourage us to believe in miracles. Loaves and fishes multiplied to feed the crowd. Blood into wine. Millions of people believe in that verbatim. Why not invest this thing with a power to change us with its symbols, its expressions, something quite real by comparison? It need not be holy.

But it is tonight.

So far, my wand got John a home and a bed, a bottle and a broad. Just like he asked. What's God got that I don't got? A following, that's what. And, incidentally, his very own universe.

It's an expresser of human magic, that's all, and it means "believe in something," such as that magic itself…my own power, my own vision. And not just me. Who's out there tonight, trying to flesh out out his or her own ideas with this pen, or some other, into a picture, a word, a statement of belief?

The streetlight is glinting on the shaft. Did sparks fly off it, just then? It looks hard and strong, streamlined, jet propelled!

I get out of the van and LEAP into the middle of the street. The reflective centerline is glowing like a fantastic yellow tightrope, and stones in the asphalt gleam like stars. And the stars themselves… there they are behind the telephone wires. Is that spirit of anger and regret floating towards us yet, anticipating our future slothful death? I see only the glare of the nearby city reflected on those Santa Monica clouds. How wonderfully clear is the black sky in between?

The wand is MY wand, now tracing a counterpoint as I dance to the spirit, balancing on a tightrope between uncertainties. Man, or child, or woman or mushroom? What am I to be? Do I live in the dark and feed on bullshit? Or am I gathering ideas from brains everywhere, up into this steely shaft, ready again to spew them forth like sparks or arrows or fire!

Now the thing is a rocket again, spinning sky-high and almost invisible among the telephone wires. Then down it comes, and I catch it barely. I won't throw it again. So what if I feel reverence? What if I don't want it bouncing on the pavement? Call me a fool. I am at odds with my fate.

Can this tool someday make me into a man, to really do something? My hand holds the thing softly 'tween thumb and forefinger and finds the shape of a woman in the air, now a cat, now a starship with sails to catch the ether winds.

I dance and twirl, my hands now up to the sky. My back is arched to stretch some cardboard muscles. A song beats in my brain, but any noise might scare the cats out here, and wake the living. Freedom! Can I have it? Release me from the longing for release, oh please?

That song—where's my pen when I need it?

Grow flowers, grow, in your sleepy moon-bed,
Through hours of nighttime, and think what I said:
That all over town is a feeling of hope,
Asleep in the dark, in your own fevered heads.

Catgut, catgut, catgut yer tongue.
Cut it out, cut it out, while yer still young.
It's better to know what you'd say and be mute.
Than fear every moment what arrow you'd shoot!

Somewhere a doggerel barked! My pen is ready to destroy!
Straighten up, to full gush. I'm doing chin-ups on a bar stuck out from a telephone pole. What a reverie, what a moment. Oh, what the hell. Calm down.

Time for a walk around the block. The little patios are lined with black fences and thorny bushes. The curtains are drawn behind the windows. I am the peeper, the prowler. What will I tell the cops when they stop me? Hey, I live a block away!

OK to walk at night, right? I'm not the *most* crazy.

It's hard for me to imagine a person who could be totally unselfconscious, walking at night among the apartments, or even in fields under stars. The isolation is so complete, who would not hear voices?

Who's behind those curtains, I wonder. A flash of flesh. The glow of late-night TV turns a curtain into a second screen. Plato's shadows jump from within the cave this time, but the flickering within is starting to flicker out.

A fire hydrant. Can I balance on it? Will I fall and castrate myself? Stepping up on one foot, I'm Mercury, poised in flight with wings on my feet. Huzzah! I'm a hood ornament.

The wand-pen comes from my pocket, into my fingers, once again an object of intense interest. Who made this thing? A craftsman? No. More likely a lowly machine chunking out its stamp, following the dull control of an automaton who's ready for lunch. There are no rings from a lathe, or maybe a hint. It's an extrusion, I realize, from hot metal.

But maybe it's a figment, a spare part from the innards of a machine, now outmoded and reused. Perhaps it was just a piece of a puzzle, nothing without its counterparts. Imagine the lead of a pencil without the wood. The turn-signal lever without the car and driver. To what possible use could those be put?

Perhaps once it was such a component in a system, a delicate lever that sets wheels in motion, a needle to point new highs. It could even have been a drumstick that banged out a child's rhythm on a plastic drum.

Now it is a pen, and yet still all of what it might have been. My wand is even now a system within a system unbuilt.

Back up upon the fire hydrant I go, proud possessor of this tool, this symbol of our mind's potential greatness. Holding up the metal stick—for it is no more than that—I now declare for all cats to hear: Take my wand, and let it bear fruit!

A voice laughs from a nearby patio, a derisive man's laugh. No, I'm caught! I'm seen! Somehow, I stay upright. It's funny how that line sounded. I laugh like a madman in return. HeeHEE, heeHAA! A shriek. But still I am on my hydrant, a burning fire of hope and craziness, wondering if my bonds have been loosed, whether my vision is clear and hope will endure, and confidence will not be so passing but something to have confidence in. Can't it one day be something to lean on please, my own vision, my own sense of worth?

My foot is killing me, standing on this unbounding water main. The snickering from the patio has stopped. I leap down, silent like a cat burglar again, pausing on the grassy verge. Listen. There is still someone in the patio. I snake back to the van, slither up into the seat. Find the key, find the key. Gun the engine, I'm gone.

TEN

THE TV STATION LOOKS just like it did last night, but what a long time ago that was. The chain link fence around the parking lot has razor wire on top. I sit out front in the van for a minute.

Finally, I drive up to the guard gate; the soldier on duty is almost asleep.

"Hi, I was supposed to meet Janda here an hour ago. Have you seen her?" The guy looks at me like he's got a toothpick in his eye.

"She wasn't expecting nobody. She left."

"Damn. Sounds like she didn't get my message. I'm her lawyer and she needs to talk to me—but don't tell that to anybody, OK? Where is she now?"

"She's got a brain. Probably sleeping."

"Look, I really need to see her, and she needs to see me, I can tell you that.

"You don't look like a lawyer. Get out of here."

"Hey. She likes unconventional people, you know that." My sarcasm misses the mark.

"Hasn't she ever asked you for good ideas? Doesn't she draw that out of you? She impresses me that way. I think she's a very special individual who needs help right now. Don't you think so?"

My lucky guess may have worked. He softens.

"You see that in her, too?"

I nod. The man is maybe 50 and solid. He was probably in the Army and a gun fell on him.

He continues:

"She's a wonderful lady. Big!" We smile. She is big, that's true.

"So what do you say? Any other ideas where she might be tonight?"

"You really her lawyer? Lemme see a card."

"I'm not her lawyer. I'm one of her partners." It's a bit of a leap, but not much.

"I was just here last night and believe me, she'll want to see me. She could probably use the support, right?"

"Sure looked that way when I saw her. I'll tell you what: I believe her gang is with her at Dollarz on Melrose. It's their late-night hangout. I went there once with 'em. Give her my regards, will ya?"

The place has dollar signs by the front door in place of lions. That's funny on a street known for its left-wing fashion sense.

By now it's about 1 a.m., still prime time for some of the crowd, but I have no hope I'll see anybody here, let alone the queen bee.

The bar and cafe is Spartan with white stucco walls, wild art, blond wood, industrial pipes painted gaudy colors for railings. Plants. I could get comfortable.

I walk room to room. The bar is quite busy with late-night jockeying for position at the finish line. It's an intense crowd of creative types. No sign of anyone I know. A row of five TV's behind the bar is playing abstract visuals without sound—moving paintings, synchronized set to set.

I wander into back rooms; tables still have some plates from dinner.

Reaching the corner, past the Ladies Room—there she is, just emerging. She's got her hand on the door, looking at the floor as if she forgot something. She looks up, suddenly aware I'm looking at her. She doesn't recognize me, I can tell.

"Chris, Chris Walkman."

My heart is POUNDING. I extend my hand for a shake. "Fancy meeting you here," I say.

Her memory has come back. I'm not sure she's too happy to see me. "I presume you recall our meeting last night?"

"Yes, Mr. Walkman, I do. It was very interesting. I enjoyed looking at your Window project. It doesn't seem we'll be able to use it anytime soon."

"That's not why I'm here, Janda."

She makes a small smile that tells me she is very tired. I'm suddenly hit with guilt to be bothering her here. But, tough! This is an important meeting.

From somewhere, I find in her exhaustion and my own anger, frustration and emotion a new surge of confidence, which might as well be drug-induced for all the permanence I expect from it. But I need a rush right now.

"Janda, me not trying to be a nuisance; but I want to talk to you about a number of things. Can I buy you a hot cocoa?"

What a dumb thing to suggest! I try again. "How about a Brandy?"

Not much better. I keep going.

"I've got questions to ask you, and things to say."

"Chris, I can't right now. My people are here, in a room. We're talking. It's been a very long day."

"I WANT to sit with you for a minute." My emotion surprises me, as if it's been lurking in my throat.

I just look at her face, behind which this unique and strong woman is deciding what to do. It's wonderful just to look at her again. I probably want her as a mother, but I feel very fatherly right now, which is also unlike me.

She turns and walks away without saying a thing. How rude! I follow her immediately, thinking maybe she'll stop and sit or say something. We pass empty tables where she could stop; we go past the bar. We come to a door at the back of the place. She opens it and I can see a table with beer bottles on it and wine and some plates. Some people are there, suddenly looking at me. I can barely face the thought of sitting in there with all of them. Roughly I pull the door shut again, in front of her. A hyena is loose in me.

She hisses: "I'm sorry, Mr. Walkman! Would you excuse me, I have a meeting going on here with some people that I MUST RETURN TO!"

"What's going on? I wanted to talk to YOU for a minute."

The strength in this woman is a little scary. Her size too. She must be an inch or two taller than me at least. And she's quite emotional herself now. She was so smooth the other night. And so was I. Now I've challenged a lioness.

My hand is on the door. I push my hair back from my forehead and take a breath. Somehow, I stand my ground. Things get even crazier.

"Janda, this is ridiculous for me to say, but I may be in love with you." She looks like she's about to spit.

"I just thought I'd tell you that. I don't recall it ever happening to me before."

"That is not of great concern to me. Tell your doctor about it. If you haven't got one, get one! Now if you'll excuse me."

"Look, forget I said it. You've got no idea who the hell I am, really, and you're too tall for me, anyway."

"I'd say YOU'RE too SHORT for ME!" She almost smiles.

I stand up much straighter.

"I'm six feet tall. But I'm trying on a Napoleon complex anyway."

Now she does smile, but it's not a very nice smile. Then she just stands there for a minute. Her head drops lower on her shoulders a little.

"I'll come in," I say.

"You'll come in." It's not a question. Then the energy returns to her, some of her realness, and some calm. I think maybe she's still furious. How could I say that I love her? The thought had barely crossed my mind. This is a business relationship!

"I promise to be a help."

She's leaning against the door, looking spectacular with her brown hair and eyes.

She says, "Yes, do not be trouble, please. This is a divided group right now."

The door opens behind her, someone from inside pulling. She steps back and lets me go in first. Great. The harsh moment has gone under the surface someplace. Now I just have to deal with the room, when the names of the people will escape me. Great boost to the confidence.

I suddenly see inside the door—to the left, that Ivan and Petra are there, which I didn't expect at all! That's awkward. Petra has got her foot up on the chair, almost underneath her, which looks like stress. Ivan is straight in his chair. They are both looking up at me, and suddenly I feel disembodied, as if I'm looking at them through a fish-eye lens.

"Hiya," I say. "C'mon give me a hug." They stand and do it, and I feel better for asking. It really is great to see them, despite their leaving today.

"How was the parade?" I ask. It's a dumb question I know.

Ivan says, "I feel sure you know how it was, Chris. It was very exciting, and now, embarrassing."

They sit down again.

Kenji Komo is there. I guess he must have gotten out on a bond or something.

"Hello, Kenji. Chris Walkman. We met last night. Nice to see you again. Exciting day today!"

"Yes, indeed. Now I am a jailbird!"

"Was it worth it?"

"I think so, though not all of us agree exactly. Will you stay for a moment?"

"I intend to."

Janda says, "Chris, I think you also met Jeff Down, who is interested in the oil platform issue."

Jeff is looking wilder today than he did at the TV station. His curly orange hair is almost standing up.

"And Tony Amboy, our physics genius. Tony is actually the one who designed the mirrors, which I presume you saw in action?"

"I saw the Hollywood Bowl performance," I admit. "I only saw your adventure Downtown on the news tonight. On KWIL. Do you know what they said about you, Janda?"

"We watched it."

"I was very angry with your mates. The Times didn't even know you were involved. Your own people broke the news that the station news director was there and made the station look sick."

Sorry Janda, I think. I guess that might be considered an insult.

"Was that just internal station politics?"

"Something like that," Kenji says.

I look around the room at the bunch. They are very different from the dramatic troop that made its creative and mysterious performance for my benefit Saturday night by the Watts Metro station and UCLA. I can only figure that was to impress me. Tonight, they look very mortal.

"Mostly, I was furious with you folks, to be honest," I further confess.

"Chris, you should join our debate, I guess," says Janda.

I continue to survey the room. I rarely get a moment like this where I feel in control and actually capable of leadership. Usually, the moment fades into the mud fairly soon. This time's gonna be different, I hope. I recall my dynamic position standing on the fire hydrant. That might help for a while.

"Thank you for the invitation. I imagine everyone's ready for bed?"

Janda says, "No rush."

"What's the debate?" Seems like a fairly basic question. Tony Amboy speaks up right away.

"It boils down to this. Activism or cooperative action? We've got a lot of energy and ideas now in this team. Many of the group are not even here."

"I miss Karin Stoney and the Dream Balloon. (???) I presume she is not into this debate at all."

Tony continues, "Right Chris, some of us are very interested in making certain public statements right now, as we did today. Some of us want to pursue other cooperative programs, in conjunction with corporate America for instance. To put it bluntly, we cannot quite agree which way to go. The result is the embarrassment of today."

"Who's been getting that Knights of the Sun group together? Kenji, that's yours, I gather?"

"Yes it is, Mr. Walkman."

"How did you get 17,000 people to head downtown after that meeting? That was an incredible feat, logistically speaking.

Kenji says, without blinking: "Buses."

Everyone laughs, and I can tell it feels good. I sit down in a chair; everyone else does too. There's a carafe of wine in the middle of the table, directors' chairs for all. I pour a glass, trying to be cool, deliberate. I'm determined to take a front-line position and stay there. It's a personal goal.

Kenji continues, "If you had seen our three earlier broadcasts, everyone knew what was on the agenda. Yesterday, we just continued the party after the morning show was over, with some premeditation obviously. However, it did not remain quite as controlled as we expected. The spirit moved us to more action, and the heat of the sun compounded the problem, with real damage to the sign and the building."

"I imagine your following has been shaken by the reaction?"

"Somewhat, but with some of the people, the commitment is actually stronger now. It had a polarizing effect, if you'll pardon the pun."

"What is the central message, the central idea of your group Kenji."

Jeff Down pipes in for the first time: "The message is simple. We can't have any more fossil fuels. The Greenhouse, its coming."

"Does that issue really motivate people to action as strongly as it seemed to, today?"

Petra suddenly speaks out, and I can tell that she is also somewhat emotional about it. I might have guessed.

"Chris, you may not be able to understand, but this company, Modern Oil, is a symbol of our country's refusal to admit what's happening. The oceans are in danger from spills. Our air and our very planet are in danger from a growing greenhouse effect that may one day destroy the home we inhabit! You know all this very well."

"We presented that idea at the Window," I remind.

"The stated goal of Knights of the Sun is to pursue natural energy sources that will not harm the Earth, and make the corporations aware of the responsibility they must bear for solving the problem! The message we sent today was clear to them.

"And they knew it was coming," she emphasizes.

This firecracker almost takes my breath away. A woman with fire in her style has been turned up to high.

"Ivan," I ask; "Did you both join this group today, with equal enthusiasm?" It's only been hours since I saw them last.

"Chris," Ivan says, "I do not think this message is so different from the one we presented through The Window. It hit on a broader media front. We felt good about it today."

"How many were actually arrested?"

"Less than a dozen," Tony says. "Who here?"

Petra and Ivan raise their hands, and Jeff—that's all. For me it's time to make a statement.

"God dammit, I think this is crazy, and stupid!" I slam my glass down on the table just hard enough for some wine to splash out. Good.

"You get some half-baked protest going—pun intended—on a SUNDAY for Christ's sake, melt part of a building sign and who knows what else, probably get Janda fired from her job, so you've got not much left. What's the big idea here? *Is* there a big idea?"

Janda says, "Chris, you are now fully integrated into our discussion."

I look at the faces around, and my sense of tiredness has come back. It's not clear that my outburst has done more than make me feel pretty good. More wine!

Janda summarizes again. "We're all asking these questions. The following of supporters that Kenji has got is excellent, not to mention the funds he is generating to support solar research and so on. It's clear there is deep support for this questioning, and even for confrontation on this issue. Certainly, we got some attention today. Direct action can be very effective. But personally, I believe we can do so much more without destruction or violence."

She pauses.

"Jeff and Kenji do not agree," she says. She's looking at them.

For the first time, I realize that this fairly tight group of people may be at a breaking point. Kenji and Jeff Down have pushed things quite far.

"My father was a credible warrior for the emperor," Kenji says. It sounds like a drone almost. "I will be one for the earth."

"Cut the dramatics, Kenji; that's a bunch of bull," I say. "What will you do without your TV network base? Surely that's gone? And even more to your point, how can Modern Oil possibly allow a group that attacked their building today to remain on the air?"

Benji summons his patience. "My congregation helps pay my bill to the station, and believe me it is not cheap. This afternoon, I had a conversation with KWIL's business manager, and with the head of Modern Oil's new Communications Unit, which is what manages the station. I made it clear to them that the events of today were an unfortunate mistake. The show will be off the air for two weeks, and I will make a public statement explaining the accident. We only meant to 'focus attention' on the company, you see."

He sounds vaguely sinister again—certainly calculating.

"In short, I will be staying on at the station. Our power base has not been disrupted."

The hyena is back in me.

"Let me make one thing clear. The thing that impressed me the most about you folks when I saw you was your strong message about creativity, building new solutions and new ideas. You have gathered idea makers, artists, planners, thinkers. That message seemed so POSITIVE. It is a CRIME to subvert that with mere protests, as creative as they may be with the mirrors and all. Why concentrate on that? What's happening? You are putting a very powerful base of action at risk; I don't care what you say about an apology."

Is smoke coming out of my ears? Jandra speaks again to explain:

"The creativity stuff was an idea from the top, ever since Modern Oil bought the station a year ago. 'Try some things with the weekend slot,' is what the station manager was told, and he told me. We're doing it. I came from Art School, and I had never really been in TV news before, but so far they like what we've been doing.

She continued: "Kenji's inspirational show sounded interesting, and we've had only a few complaints. His success has been a big motivator for all of us, actually. I think Kenji's got some staying power. Modern Oil will not want to risk the anger from Kenji's group if he is dropped from the schedule so quickly, when all is explained as a misunderstanding. My guess is that, despite the big scene they made yesterday, Modern Oil will accept apologies and drop the charges."

"So, would you do it again if you had the chance?" I ask, with some emotion.

"We would watch out for the damage," Jeff says, apparently in a minor concession to my sudden vehemence. "Those mirrors surprised even Tony. Right, Tony?"

"Look, let's cut the charade," Tony says. "The fact of the matter is we knew perfectly well the mirrors might cause damage. I couldn't tell how much. The hotness of the day made it worse. But of course we should claim surprise, that it was an accident."

He sounds disgusted. Almost to himself he says, "We really did a job on that sign."

Jeff regains his righteousness. "I'm not even that interested in the apology, particularly. Think of all the damage this company has done to the earth, to the city. They have got to take responsibility."

Janda says, "After last night, I think I know what Chris would say. Who's taking responsibility for driving the cars? Who's buying the gas? We are!"

"It's a question of leadership," Jeff responds. "Someone has got to step up and step out of line to break the habits. It was big corporate America that got rid of the Red Car trolleys in Los Angeles so they could promote cars. Who's capable of making a change of that magnitude again? Them! The companies have got to be *encouraged*."

"But KWIL is doing something, encouraging creative programming on their station, right?"

Janda says, "Let's don't overstate the case here, OK. They say they are diversifying, but it really boils down to a very simple idea. Promote Modern Oil product in this market. I got a specific mandate to try things on weekend days and nights. They think it improves ratings, and I think Ned Garder, the chairman, likes to look like an innovator or something. I've talked to him. He's a bit of a grandstander. But they are experimenting with image mongering, something only a 30-billion-dollar company could do.

"If you want to know the truth, our approach to creative programming is pretty much an accident, trying out a few segments on the environment, homelessness and so on. We're just getting going, and we've had some chances to make a few mistakes,. But this thing today was pushing it."

"Where is this going for them?" I ask.

"I think they may be considering offers on other TV stations in major markets.

Their marketing people seem convinced that they can really save on their advertising budget, especially if the station breaks even or better. They've got an entire new division devoted to the idea, Modern Comm they call it. Anyway, that expansion information is very secret right now. I think the fact we know it may be helping to save my job. Keep it to yourself, please."

"Where is the FCC in this?"

"Modern Oil will make disclosures when they have to, before the purchases. They're not doing anything yet."

I take a deep breath. This was a lot I didn't know.

Blurting out I say, "Janda, what you just said confirms my feeling that this confrontation idea just doesn't make any sense at all. Without knowing it, Modern Oil is doing something good here with this station. More than that, if it's cultivated, it could be outstanding. I've not had a chance to talk with you further about Wand Enterprises.

"So listen, folks; here's my idea. Janda: I can see your ambivalence about this violence thing.

"Kenji, and Jeff, and my apologies to Petra—I think you should leave this group."

Everybody looks at me like I've just fired a gun. It's quite exciting.

"You folks have got a beef with Modern Oil, which is clear. I just don't think you should be operating with the likes of Janda and her team of other great people. For my money, keep your religious show going, great. But get the hell out of her way. Do not jeopardize the evolution of a really great base to try new programming and so on by pissing people off. Janda, you agree, I know."

I'm standing up, really trying to drive this situation, sounding like a first-class tyrant. One more second and I'll point my finger at the door.

Janda is not happy with me at all. I bet when the air is clear, she'll feel better.

Petra is livid, but Kenji is not that easy to intimidate.

"Janda, this interloper is trying to reshape our group," he says. "Do you agree with his ultimatum?"

She is silent for a minute. I think it will take all her remaining energy to answer this question. She looks at Kenji, Jeff, and finally at Petra.

"I agree with Chris. You should not be a part of our creative works. You are part of the station, with your show. I will not try to end that. But I must cease the connection between you and News, and the creative shows. The risk is too great, and the ethics are not so hot either. Goodbye Kenji and Jeff. Ivan and Petra, your future is your own to decide."

Kenji and Jeff stand up, and look without anger at Janda. She says, "Who knows, we may still benefit in other areas from your motivating power."

Kenji does a quick bow, which I think is almost funny. Then they walk out the door. The group is split.

Janda looks at me with a grim face. "Who the hell are you to influence me!" she seems to shout.

Me, I'm just a guy who's trying to find his voice. This has been a great practice session.

The wand is in my pocket, a good luck omen.

ELEVEN

MORNING HAS COME. A sun-shadow once again makes a pattern on the wall, filtered through plants and my half-open eyes. I went to bed at 3. Now it's 7. The cat came back last night. She's on my chest. We're going back to sleep for a while.

The sun shadow now is on the floor. What's it, 9 or something? Much better. It's Monday, what sort of a day is this for working? I've been at it all weekend.

The good news from last night stays with me. Today I'll take the equipment for the Window project back to the rental store. Then head on to the station again. I've got a meeting with Janda at 11. What a great big gal. All's fun again in sunny Los Las.

The queen bee was too tired to argue at the end of the evening. It was a tough session and she didn't want to admit it, but I did some dirty work for her. Got the bad apples out of the barrel. Now we can concentrate on the creative, the growing, the new ideas, forget the confrontation.

Modern Oil is obviously ready to allow experimentation with the TV station. Jandra's got a great outfit there. We can take The Window to a wider audience now; burst into some new areas, cut through the barriers, use the news and two-way interaction like a lens into problems, a presenter of solutions, a Wand.

I sit up in bed, feeling the excitement all over again. It's a new day. Oh, courage, oh confidence, love it while it's here!

I really don't think Kenji took it too badly. He's still got his program and Janda will benefit from it. It's probably a good group behind him that believes in the new and the hopeful. But Kenji just wanted to take that someplace wrong. Janda knew it. She just couldn't admit it.

Now the good guys are ready to roll. It's so great that Ivan is on board, he's a real talent. The Window could not have happened without him. I'm excited that our team's going to be back in action again. Gotta call John later. But poor Petra, she's the one I felt for. She wouldn't leave Ivan, but she really sided with Kenji, I think. She was definitely over a rail. But I'll take my leverage where I can find it.

Brush brush those slimy teeth. And shave shave shave those whiskers away. Down the dark drain tunnel they go, way away to the sea. Sickening.

What if everyone had to keep their household wastewater right on their premises? Wait until trucks could come and get it. Boy that would solve the water shortage in L.A. Right away. I understand there are experiments with recycling "grey water." Great idea.

And I'll suggest my other show idea to Janda, "Our Gangs," about the gangs and their logos, and so on.

But now's the time for some orange juice and Grape Nuts and my beloved L.A. Times, awaiting me even now on my doorstep where it's been browning lightly in the SoCal sun.

Some cartoons on TV for background? I'll pass today.

And lookit, the Knights of the Sun even made the front page with photograph and story. Let's see how Mr. Mosley handled the issue.

SUN WORSHIPPERS
'ACCIDENTALLY' DAMAGE
M-OIL HQ WITH MIRRORS

LEADERS ENCOURAGED VIOLENCE, INSIDER SAYS

Story by Dan Mosey, staff writer:
Some 10,000 mirror-wielding members of the increasingly radical environmental group Knights of the Sun inflicted significant

damage to the downtown headquarters building of the Modern Oil Company just after noon Sunday by focusing rays of the sun on the building's sign and upper floors. Portions of the company's sign were melted.

The leader of the protest, Kenji Komo, a martial arts specialist and activist, told reporters, police and representatives of Modern Oil that the incident was an "unfortunate mistake."

"Our intention," Komo said, "was merely to shine our light on a problem that the company is well aware of: the need to increase research into renewable energy sources such as solar energy, and to reduce the impact on our atmosphere of burning fossil fuels. None of us wants to see the Earth die in the coming greenhouse.

"We extend our deep regrets to the management of Modern Oil Company for the property damage. It was accidental, a miscalculation."

"Komo and two other people were arrested and held briefly, charged with unlawful assembly and destruction of property. Initially, Modern Oil executives on the scene vowed to press charges.

"Company chairman Ned Garder, who came to inspect the damage personally, said: 'If upon investigation we determine that there was no malice intended, we will review our thinking. Certainly, it's difficult to fault the sincerity of the group.'

"The Times has learned, however, that the event may have been carefully planned with the cooperation of members of the news team at local station KWIL Channel 8, which is owned by the oil company. KWIL news personnel stated this on the 11 p.m. broadcast last night, though no one at the station would confirm the statement for a caller.

"A source close to the protest said that weekend news director Janda Evers supported the action and the resulting damage to "encourage people to do the right thing." The source said the planning included the possibility of inflicting damage.

"Evers is a close associate of Mr. Komo, and was with him the night before the event, the source said.

"The attack is at least an embarrassment to Modern Oil which recently acquired the station and has experimented with a variety of programming changes there. In a further irony, the Knights of the

Sun had earlier in the morning conducted a ritual mirror ceremony at the Hollywood Bowl that was televised on KWIL.

"No senior management at the station or at Modern Oil were available to comment on the late-breaking development."

Uh-oh. My Grape Nuts are no longer edible. My stomach is in a little knot the size of a golf ball. Janda may not be my friend this morning.

I lock up the house. I don't want to take the time, but I've got to take the video equipment back to the rental store. As I expected, the last of the money from Hugo will go to pay the balance due.

The van goes back to U-Haul, where I pick up my Toyota. The clutch feels very weird. The clutch I'm in, I mean.

Eleven a.m. at KWIL, it's the first time I've been there during the day. The guard from the gate last night is working the front desk now. I'd hate to be in security. You're always the victim of sadistic schedulers.

He's got the Times open to the inside page of the story. It's caught everyone's eye, I'll bet. Maybe I'll be lucky and stay an unknown, unnamed source. I'm not usually that lucky.

"Hiya, Mr. Lawyer. Did you ever get to our lady last night?"

"Perfect, thanks. Have you seen her today?"

"Not since she came in looking like the angel of death. What'd you guys drink last night?"

"Bitters. Look, Sam (it's on his badge), I'm supposed to meet with Janda now, right here. I've got an appointment, believe it or not. Can I go on in?"

"Hold it, I'll ring."

Despite his war wounds, he dials the number from memory. I'm impressed.

He coos into the phone with a lady he must like.

"Hello, it's me. We have a visitor for Janda. Is she seeing anyone yet? That's what I thought. Yeah, Mr....," looking at me: "What's your name again...?"

"Walkman, Chris Walkman."

"A mister Chris Walkman is here for a meeting with Janda. Yeah, OK, I'll warn him." He hangs up with a ding.

"As I thought; if you're ready for a stiff greeting, go right on ahead! Straight in the front door, then first right."

"Thanks. I hope your head feels better." Dumb thing to say.

The smell of dying roses has been replaced with something more like cleaning solvent. Walk through the swinging doors. Head into the recovery ward.

Turn right into the office of Janda. I never did see it the other night, only the screening and editing room. I've lost my bearings this time, not sure in which room I met the creative group.

Janda looks dark and dangerous. She's sitting at her desk, L.A. Times in front of her, hands on either side of the paper. She looks like she sucked in a breath 20 minutes ago and hasn't let go yet. It's a scary sight. My mind is working overtime to figure a way out of this. I'm anticipating the worst and I shouldn't. It's not clear to me she even knows I was the source.

"You son of a bitch."

I think she knows I was the source. "Miss-quoted," I say.

"Miss-quote bullshit, you fucking busybody. You told me last night the Times didn't even know I was involved." She slaps the paper. "This guy heard you just about the way I did. So much for trusting a potential partner. You sure know how to lend a hand!"

She puts her forehead down on the table. I wonder if she's been crying, but I can't believe it—just dramatics. Boxes are piled on the floor.

"Are you moving?"

"You son of a bitch." The S makes the most noise. "As of last night, Modern was ready to stay with the station. I said before, we made a mistake; we knew it. We went right up to the edge, we looked over. Even this morning we were OK; we pulled it off. Now we're off the cliff.

Her voice gets quieter and quieter, as if she's moving back to the end of a tunnel and whispering is all that's allowed.

"Chairman Garder called me at home this morning and asked personally for my resignation. And he has personally killed Kenji's show, despite the thousands of dollars it might represent, and the good besides."

She spins her head at me, and I'm a dartboard.

"You did it Chris. You convinced them we meant harm and were trying to embarrass them."

I'm trying to remember what that confidence this morning felt like. It's gone like horse from barn. Boy, it's hard to find a reasonable response when necessary.

"I'm sorry, Janda. There is so much to say, but I can't say anything. I'm sorry." Never apologize, somebody told me.

"Chris, let me just explain, so you'll understand. I came here to the station, the news department, because Modern Oil was ready for some changes. This was so ideal. So perfect. Such a great place to try stuff!

"You know. You saw everybody. It's a great bunch of people have come here. I love that creation piece. We ran it one time."

"Janda, answer me this. Why did you put it all at risk anyway? Why did you confront Modern? It makes no sense to me. You knew I didn't like the threat of violence. Yeah, I talked to the damn reporter. What he didn't catch was the disappointment."

Now, I'm the earnest one. I should be pissed, or self-righteous, and I guess I am. At myself, for screwing this up. But at her, too, because she screwed it up too. I just didn't let her get away with her mistake.

"Chris, I said we pushed it to the edge. We meant it. We meant to. Part of it was like I said last night. The new division of Modern Oil they see as a marketing tool and that's about all. We wanted to drive that group even farther, because we believe at least some activism was necessary to make these station changes work. I mean we can do public affairs shows all day long, drive our audience share into the dirt and go out of business. Frankly that's a good way *not* to succeed. We wanted to be provocative, to raise some hackles and really attract attention." She shakes her head, struggling with it.

"What you saw last night, you know, when the anchor pointed out that I was involved? Garder already knew. He probably knew we were coming over to his building yesterday. We've been pushing for a more activist role for weeks as we shake this new thing out. But he's just not going for it. We thought that little demonstration would liven things up a little bit."

This is true confessions.

"What you did, Chris, is leave him no room to maneuver. For public consumption, we had it as a mistake. You made it into an act of defiance, and he couldn't have it."

Now, I'm coming up to speed. "You're saying that the march yesterday was both demonstration project, to show the power of activism, plus a real call for more solar power?"

"And it was a hot day," she explains, "so we got more damage out of our mirrors than we bargained for."

"So, what'll happen to all these people you brought in, their great ideas?" She rolls her eyes.

"Mr. Guy, it's all kaputski. I hope you feel proud. You can't imagine how furious Garder was."

"You talked to him directly?"

"He called me. I was getting to be a favorite. But that guy is so wild, I'm enemy number one right now, and Kenji's number two. He said they're even stopping their looking at the other stations. He's bringing it all to a stop.

She shakes her head.

"Don't you feel powerful, Chris? Just a single comment, you change the world!"

The irony of that does not escape me. But it's all wrong. Why should such good intentions come to an end so fast?

"Janda, I feel like some demon force that turns everything to dust. But, this is insane. How could all the energy of the station, and Modern, and you and Kenji, and your people—all evaporate into nothing? It just doesn't seem possible, or fair. Does it?"

"It's what happens when forces balance just right," she says. "Pull the right card, and all of them come down at once. It's the way history works."

I suddenly realize that she's not mad right now and she's been calm for several minutes. I think I'm falling in love again, or it's that paternal instinct.

"Where will you go?"

"I've got no concept right now."

"Will you hook up with your people you brought to the station? I thought they were a great bunch."

"I'll help 'em along, but I was in this for the TV station. Now that we're on our own, they can handle themselves and I'll stay in touch.

"How about Kenji?"

"Same. But you really did clear my mind on him last night. I was looking forward to a less confrontational approach. He and Jeff were too far out on the edge. After you were so strong on the point, I decided I agreed. We could have done growth and creativity without confrontation." She sighs.

"What will Kenji do, and Jeff?"

"He's got his organization, and he might be worth money to some station that will pick him up, if any would. That's open to question, actually."

She sits quietly, hands between her legs like she's keeping warm or considering a return to the womb. She stares at the newspaper. I'm still standing in front of her desk like it's been some audience with the Pope. I sit down with a plunk in a chair. We're in neutral for a minute.

"You're big for me, but I do love you, I think."

Such passion. She looks up like she didn't hear me.

"You should consider a career in politics, Mr. Chris. You've got a way with words."

"No really, you're so big and strong.

"Thanks anyway."

"What are you doing for lunch? It's about that time."

"Forget it. I'm out of here. I'm going home. I'll see you later. I'm not talking anymore." Suddenly she's closing up like a clam. I think she did go back to the womb.

"Well, what will happen to your people? You still haven't told me?"

"Here, you take 'em."

She hands me a typewritten sheet with names, addresses, and phone numbers. She says, "I'm not their mother."

"Well, damn it, I thought you sort of were. Is no one going to try to keep this thing going? Who do I have to talk to get this program back in development, on the air?"

"You're wasting your time. Brandon said he's out of the good-deed business."

I pull my wand-pen from my pocket, feeling a little desperate.

"Janda, I'm going to get your job back, in the name of Wand Enterprises." She smiles a cynical smile.

"Call me when you do. My number is on the sheet there. Visit the general manager if you want, Bob Zemlin. See what you can do. I think you'll find he's delighted about the change. Now he can get to work on those ratings. Sweeps are coming up; gotta get some jiggle on there."

The cynicism is more than alarming. A central figure in my life, a kind of beacon, is fading. A dream of new possibilities in creativity, in hope, in daring new thought, all of which this woman seemed to embody in just herself, is fading, as if it never existed; and so is my hope for Wand Enterprises, an idea that was just getting stronger.

"C'mon, listen. Even if the station isn't here, and isn't a backdrop, we can do something with all those people, with that spirit I saw. You showed me some great people. I want to get this Wand Industries going! I need your help!"

She's got her bag over her shoulder, and two boxes stacked in front of her.

"Goodbye Chris. See Zemlin, talk him into it."

She's walking out the door, past me; I'm stunned. She's out into the hall, into the lobby, past the front desk, to the parking lot. I'm following lamely behind, along with nobody else. Her fellow employees don't even look; a plague victim is passing.

I call out, "Wand, it's going to happen. You should be part of it."

"Mr. Zemlin is inside, to the left. He's your man."

She lowers the boxes into the back seat of a Mercedes, '83 or something. Slams the door. Opens the front with a shake and rattle of her key. Looks at me.

"Very best of luck to you. Call me when you've got my job back. I'll be delighted to talk with you."

She drives away.

I'm devastated, standing by her car, then watching it go. I sit down on the curb and cry, cry, cry, looking at the grains of sand moved up against the parking block, a gum wrapper, a cigarette butt. A column of ants busily hefts grains of sand back and forth, all absorbed in their chores, aligned unquestioningly to the benefit of all.

Then, I do go back into the station, find the General Manager's office. Walk in past secretary who says, yes, may I help you…wait!" as I walk past.

I sit in a chair before Zemlin's paper-covered desk and begin talking.

"Hi, I'm Chris Walkman and I wanted to introduce myself."

At least he's looking at me.

"The loss of Janda here is critical. So is the loss of the Modern Oil support, and the creative, problem-solving programming you were able to do. I think this is a disaster of major proportions, for our city, our country and the earth, simply because it was a revolutionary idea that deserved a chance to work. I'm here to do anything I can to make this work, to give it another chance. Where can I start?" Took a breath.

He sits back in his chair, looks at his secretary who has followed me as far as the door. It's OK, I'll deal with the lunatic.

"Ah, Mr. Walkman."

The room is quiet now as Zemlin slowly puts his hands behind his head, leans farther back, flares out his elbows and adopts a sly sneer on his face. He's biting a short pencil. I'm reminded of a cobra, and the pencil looks like his tongue. I've always wondered if that hands-behind-head routine is body language that says, "I'm a snake. I'm afraid of you so don't get too close. See how big I am?"

He says, "Mr. Walkman, our friend. So YOU are the helpful person who was in touch with the local paper last night. Am I right about that?"

"Mr. Zemlin, I can only say to you what I should have said then: No comment."

"Well, you should know that that time-worn phrase is very often a very stupid thing to say to the press. Anything you'd like to say instead?"

What a jerk. A smart jerk, though.

"I told Janda just now, just before she left"—he raises his eyebrows; he didn't know she'd left so soon—"I was just expressing disappointment to the reporter, and surprise that such an exciting and creative endeavor as she was beginning would be marred by resorts to violence and stupid, self-defeating displays of hyperactive activism. In the spirit of creativity, renewal and growth, which I thought was what she was going to be concentrating on here, the attack on M-Oil did not fit and did not become her. She agreed with me, actually. She decided that Kenji would not be part of her news team any more, or Jeff."

"Well, the short version of your speech, as quoted by our LA Times friend Don Mosey here"—he holds up a folded copy of the paper—"certainly had a strong impact on our chairman, and I'm sure Janda's departure has brought that home to you."

He stops for a second and takes a drink from his coffee. The mug says "Genius at Work."

"Personally, I'm delighted," he says, waits for the effect to sink in.

"I extend my thanks to you. But I would guess that thanks are not necessary." He snorts.

He takes a breath, and then wearily lets it out as he says, "In fact, we may actually be able to make some money for our distinguished chairman, now that this social agenda and creativity folderol is behind us."

Who ever says "folderol" anymore?

Zemlin continues: "I cannot bring myself to imagine WHAT the proposed televised visits into the ghetto, and programs on solar power, and oil platforms turned into ocean museums, and garbage sculpture, would have done for our ratings. I am entirely relieved that we came to this speedy conclusion. In fact, it was my understanding all along that we were supposed to be doing marketing for Modern Oil, not solving the world's problems.

"Whatever! I didn't think it would be long before Brandon realized how his pet project was going over with company shareholders. I was not entirely delighted at the prospect of presiding over the station's further decline. Frankly, I've got some great plans for this station. For instance, we've got re-colorized versions of "The Man from Uncle" before the five o-clock news. I'm excited about it because I believe Mr. Brandon will be much more receptive to those sorts of ideas at this time. Don't you think that's got some merit in terms of celebrating a new world order, Mr. Walkman?"

I put one finger on the edge of his desk, then look back into his eyes. It's sometimes good to lock on with a staring contest.

"You make me sick."

"You've truly got a way with words, Mr. Walkman."

"Don't you have any regard for what the station could have done to address problems?"

"We have got one problem to address and I've indicated what it is: Ratings. I don't believe you can help me with that, so if you would excuse me…?"

"Who's managing this property for Modern Oil?"

"You wouldn't want to know them. I'm afraid they share my sentiments rather completely. It's Garder's new communications subsidiary, Modern Comm. It's right downtown in their newly decorated building—this one with the distinctive MELTED sign on top," pointing to the paper. "I'm sure you'll recognize it.

"By the way: be sure to let me buy you a drink one day. I owe it all to you: my new, improved almost entirely sane new future. Good day, Mr. Walkman. If you will excuse me, I have an important luncheon appointment."

I don't even want any last words. It pleases me to simply stand, turn and walk out, past the brain-damaged attendant, through the lobby, which smells like stale coffee, back to my trusty Toyota.

A limousine is pulling into the parking lot. You can never see anybody inside those things.

My car is hot inside from waiting in the sun. Sometimes that oppressive warmth is perfect when your body is chilled to the bone.

Zemlin has come out of the lobby with his sport coat on. He gets into the limo and it turns and angles back out of the parking lot, an ocean liner missing its tug boats. The black shape heads into the traffic while lesser vehicles nose around it.

Then they close up the space and he and the mystery contents are gone.

TWELVE

I FIND MYSELF THINKING about Nathan Hale, hero of the Revolutionary War. He got caught by the British and hanged as a spy in 1776, 21 years old.

Saw a picture of him once, on his way up a ladder to the noose. He supposedly said, "I regret I have but one life to give for my country." Probably some biographer made it up. But the picture in my mind is so vivid. I wonder if his honor made him step off the ladder by himself or did his knees get too weak to even climb. The guy's a hero, I can't believe the British soldiers had to drop him off.

Then I wonder about being on the end of the rope with three or four minutes to think about it. I bet you never realize how heavy you are until you're supporting your weight with your NECK. Maybe it's the finality of death that gets me, but when somebody sends you off the edge, totally against your will, that's the worst. The idea matches my state of mind.

By contrast, here's a sunny Monday afternoon on the Santa Monica Freeway, heading downtown. Am I really going anywhere? In theory, I'm going to visit the offices of Modern-Comm. A last stand.

"Dang me, oughtta take a rope and hang me!" Love that Roger Miller song.

You know, I should probably call Mr. Mosey again at the Times to complain about his damn story that's caused me such grief, but

I'd just be chasing a gone horse. I never thought about the power of the press until it's pressing on me.

I can't quite figure out what's making me the maddest right now: my own stupidity, or Janda folding up and quitting like that, or that damned station manager's smirk of glee at his liberation. I just know I feel reduced to a peon, less than a pea in the soup.

With all those forces and ideas flying around, I almost got connected to some, almost got in synch with the spheres somehow, made something big happen. Felt like we had some kind of launching pad under construction. Wand Enterprises! I think with that idea connected to the TV station somehow, we would have had some REAL leverage to change some things. I almost started to care, have some faith. Then, step on a mine, choose a few words wrong and I'm spinning in infinity, nowhere to hold on.

Hugo's stupid face comes back to me, too, reminding me that I supposedly owe him 20,000 bucks.

Dammit, I SMASH the dashboard of the car, pound my head back on the headrest. I'm a victim, but I know I'm not. I'm just one piece in the infinite machine.

Stupid wand idea, just a ballpoint pen.

The brain movie shows scientist Rod Taylor in "The Time Machine," putting the lever from his vehicle in his pocket. He's arrived at the year 802701 from 1900, long after World War Three. By then, the earth has changed a lot and most of civilization is wiped out. He wants to take a look around, why not? Little does he know about the dreaded Morlocks. But where does he park the time car? Ah, never mind. He can simply take the key to the machine—a short brass rod with a cut-glass jewel on the top.

Carefully he unscrews it from the control panel and slips it into his pocket. It's his ticket out of there, his leverage to past and future. The machine goes nowhere without it.

My time-and-hope machine is still unassembled. The pieces are the names that Janda gave me, and my names from the Window and the Sunday afternoon meeting. I can't think of any power to weld them into action, even with what I said to Janda. I'm driving downtown on empty.

The skyline is clear, like yesterday. There's the melted Modern Oil sign. I grind up the Harbor Freeway and swoop off at 6th Street, park in a no parking zone.

I realize as I get out of the car, I've got really nothing to lose. I'm caught out in the open now and my caution is gone. I feel liberated enough by failure and embarrassment to be almost dangerous. I stride into the inky inside of the grey-black Modem Oil tower, up to the marble-walled security station on the ground floor. TV monitors cast a hollow glow. A security officer lady is seated there with a headset on her head.

"I'm looking for Modern-Comm. What floor are they on? They're in this building, right?"

"Do you have a clearance sir?"

"No ma'am."

"Just wondering," she says. "29th Floor please."

The lobby there is grey with "Mod-Comm" written large on the wall in reflective chrome. Looks like an aerospace company: "Ideas in the air" or something.

Another security desk, a receptionist, a young black girl trim in a blue suit. "May I help you?"

I've got no idea where to go from here, not even a name.

"Hello, my name is Chris Walkman, I'm a big fan of your TV station KWIL. You know, I love the basketball. I just wanted to talk to someone about the crazy stuff that happened yesterday, with all those mirrors you know? And the LA Times story this morning. Is there anyone who can see me?"

"I'm sorry sir, its lunch time and no one is in the office right now." She's very polite, and no help.

"Well, I especially wanted to hear what you folks are planning there after the craziness I've seen. I'm very anxious to know whether you are going to STOP that wild man and his band of HOOLIGANS. As a Modern Oil shareholder, I'm afraid I do not think you are doing the company a service by allowing such irresponsible behavior in your operations. It's ridiculous that the station would inspire such wanton behavior and allow damage to be inflicted on its property."

"Sir, we always appreciate the views of our shareholders. To get your point across most effectively, may I suggest that you write a letter? I'll be happy to give you the address."

"Who should I write to?" I'm getting somewhere.

"We take a sincere interest in our shareholders here at Mod-Comm. You should write directly to the vice president for communications, Bradford Earnshaw, care of..."

"Is he here today?"

"Sir, I do not know."

"Is he actually responsible for the TV station?"

"Sir, Mr. Earnshaw is responsible for all the new communications efforts that Modern-Oil is beginning with Mod-Comm. However, I do not know whether Mr. Earnshaw is even going to be back from...is going to be in the office today."

That was another important tip there, but she's catching on that I'm a madman.

"Tell you what. Would it be possible for me to compose a letter right here? If I could have a sheet of paper, I could just sit on that couch over there. It would mean a lot to me to get my feelings off my chest right now, if you know what I mean?"

"I'm sorry Mr. Walkman, our lobby is not an office. I will be delighted to offer you a sheet of paper and a pen and you may visit our lobby downstairs to compose your thoughts." She tears off a sheet of yellow paper from a pad and puts it with a pen up on the edge of her little fortress.

"Thank you, thank you." I try to engage her with a convincing smile. The old charisma is not quite up to it. I take the paper over to the couch, sit down and begin writing immediately, keeping eyes down. Let her call Security. I don't think she will as I concentrate, write small, stalling for time.

It's 45 minutes before, as I expected, Bob Zemlin the station manager comes into the lobby with presumably Mr. Earnshaw who presumably was the contents of the limo. They're laughing hearty laughs. Who can fault the good old boys? Surely Mr. Earnshaw understands the value of ratings on his station. Now Mr. Zemlin has taken him through the new developments and things are looking up!

I stand up sharply as they pass into the lobby, heading for Earnshaw's office. "Hello, Mr. Zemlin, a pleasure to see you again, sir."

He stops and looks at me. "Hello, Mr. No Comment." His teeth are clenched.

"Please allow me to vote for that response from you now." It's almost a whisper of panic.

Mr. Earnshaw is not confused as to what is going on. It looks like Zemlin has explained everything.

"Hello, Mr. Earnshaw," I say. "I'm Chris Walkman, as you appear to know. It was my words that appeared in The Times this morning, which were apparently the source of some displeasure from your Mr. Garder. I make a better source in person than I do as an unnamed one, so I thought I'd introduce myself. Have you got a minute? I'd like to say a few words if you do."

He and Zemlin look at each other again. Earnshaw takes control.

"Yes, Mr. Walkman, a pleasure to meet you." His irony does not escape me. "Bob here mentioned your, ah, contribution, to our efforts with KWIL, though I understanding it was an unwitting assist, eh? Frankly, Chris, I'm not sure we have all that much to talk about. Our interests seem to conflict—though, honestly, Bob only expressed the vaguest understanding of what your interests actually are."

He takes a minute to study me. As usual, I don't make a very impressive picture with jeans and a plaid shirt. Earnshaw is a killer in pinstripe. The receding hairline reduces the intimidation factor slightly.

"I tell you what, Mr. Walkman; I'll give you five minutes to make your own case. Does that seem fair, or what?"

Bob is not happy about this, but his face is impassive. The boss has made a noble gesture; how could anyone complain?

We walk into the back office past low cubicles. Earnshaw's office is in the prestigious corner, but plain. The carpet is green, there's a glass coffee table.

Earnshaw moves slowly behind his football field of a black desk and sits down. Bob Zemlin's not too comfortable in the boss's office so he walks to the window and looks out. Then he turns and leans against the sill, folding his arms in case of trouble.

Earnshaw looks at his watch and says, "Now Mr. Walkman. Five minutes. Speak!"

What am I, a dog? Oh well, five minutes to the noose. I take a big breath.

Fight! Fight! Fight! I try to be level-headed and earnest.

"Let me say first that I don't know Janda Evers all that well. We are certainly not accomplices, if you're worried about that."

"Noooo." Earnshaw is helpful.

"Anyway, on Saturday night I brought into your station, to Janda Evers, some tapes that my associates and I created just that evening. We had conducted an experiment in crossing the gulf between two communities in our city, specifically Westwood and Watts with face-to-face video, allowing and encouraging conversation, communication and contact between these two very different neighborhoods. We think it was an innovative thing to do. We are only beginning to see the full ripple effect."

I'm standing, walking, trying to own this office. So is bulldog Bob. He wants me to be small. He sits down on the couch which serves to make him look even slinkier. Earnshaw puts his feet up on his desk, seeking forgotten lunch with a toothpick.

I'll try again to get their attention. "Gentlemen, I saw two things that night to change the world!"

They do not budge. Why should they believe me? I think I'm just confirming their suspicions.

"One thing I saw was this experiment I've described, brought to KWIL on an exclusive basis. We left off the decision just how we will air any portion of it, until you see the light. When you see it, you will realize that leaping barricades of understanding between people is something worth doing. We can do more, with our vision made of video."

Whew! I take a breath. This sort of thing is new to me.

"Perhaps you do not understand. TV news can go into the ghetto any time, or show Westwood anytime to us all. But how often do people in one area really get to converse with people in the other, face to face in an organized and conscious way?"

"It's up to me, and you, to make that happen more?"

Earnshaw's eyebrows go up: Oh yeah?

"The second miracle I saw was this. Janda had on her team some brilliant people with ideas tried almost nowhere, as of yet. I saw instantly that the drive to create, to seek and proclaim original ideas that can break the bounds of our lethargy and suffocation— that spirit was alive in her, and in her people. I've seen nothing like it anywhere else."

Death in their faces.

"Frankly, between you and me, I was devastated to be so surpassed in my own thinking by what she was preparing to do— by what YOU had already done with KWIL, Mr. Earnshaw. Janda Evers was beginning something that could save the world. I saw it that night. You have seen it too, for the station was on that course when I came, though I didn't know it before.

Damn! How can I hit them harder, and be clearer?

"Did you even know what your station was doing?"

Earnshaw's hand is over his mouth. He is ever so slightly troubled, but he's keeping this confession tightly capped. The eyebrow raises again, the hand comes off.

"Mr. Walkman, I believe you know by now that the programming experiment at KWIL that Janda was working on was encouraged by others who, frankly, did not have a large amount of expertise in television. This effort, of which you witnessed a small portion, has now been concluded. Mr. Zemlin here has new plans for the station, which I believe our senior management will welcome in the current climate of, er...corporate tension. Do you have more to say in your remaining"—looks at his watch—"two minutes?"

"Just this." And I summon all the energy of the Wand.

"Janda and her team are invited to join Wand Enterprises, which was born Saturday night, of which this magic wand is a symbol."

The eyebrows go up even higher.

"I do not say that Janda will even come, but she's a force that someone must appreciate, as I do. My own team in Wand Enterprises will join with hers. With the new ideas we asked for on Saturday night, we will change the world. But the leverage you possess in your TV station would make an enormous difference. You are stepping back. I urge you forward."

It seems possible that the spirit of Kenji Komo has entered my brain. But this is almost too scary for me. I stand up, thinking maybe I'll just walk out. Some salesman I am.

Earnshaw says, "Mr. Walkman, thank you for your passionate speech. We can certainly appreciate the depth of your commitment and I am sorry that we cannot be the partner you envision. Let me make these points before we conclude."

"I'm listening."

"First, KWIL is a business and as such must be operated with due consideration for our shareholders. In my view—and my superiors have disagreed with me until now—we have been failing in that responsibility. I am quite relieved to say the situation has changed. The purpose of the station is to make money by entertaining people, and, within the Modern Oil family, to support other activities of the company. I'm talking about the sale of petrochemical products, which is our business, after all.

"Number two, your hopes that any station can be a force for significant change are a fantasy. My experience is that people want entertainment from their TV set, not challenging ideas or unpleasantness. While that may be a sad fact, it is a fact nonetheless. I am sorry that the plans for the station changed for the reason they did—namely the actions yesterday by Janda's Raiders, as I choose to call them." There's a note of anger in his voice.

"She had nothing to do with that god damned thing!"

"Chris, that is not true and you know it. The important thing is that the station is now free to give the public what it wants, not what it needs, and that is the only way to run any business in our society. If you want state-run, socialized propaganda and thought control from your TV, there are some countries I can direct you to. Now I think that concludes our discussion."

His lips are pursed, and Zemlin's arms are folded very tightly.

"Mr. Walkman, I sincerely wish you luck and will watch your endeavors with interest. Your aims are noble. Please do not try to link them with our business."

He's gotten up from his chair, moved to the door and opened it. He is now standing to let me out into the hallway. He sticks his head out.

"Cindy, would you help Mr. Walkman find his way to the elevator, that's a good girl."

Lucky Cindy. Earnshaw is waiting for me at the door.

I move over to the desk where Earnshaw was sitting. I sit down. His desk is quite clean. The chair is still warm.

"Actually," I announce, haughtily, "I would like to make just a few more brief points. It appears to me you simply do not understand what we need to do. We need to hire Janda back, and we need to return to our earlier course."

My voice is rattling in my throat. I'm still not much of a confrontationist. Earnshaw is white.

"Bob would you come out here please?"

The two of them go out of the office and shut the door. I'm sitting at the desk, the wielder of power for a terrifying moment.

For some reason, I remember John's phone number at Judy's. I pick up the phone and dial. It rings two, three, four times.

"Hello?" It's the ice cream man himself. "John! Chris here, how the hell are ya?"

"Fine Chris. Where are you, what are you doing?"

"I'm sitting at a vice president's desk on the 29th floor of the Modern Oil Building, about to get arrested."

"Arrested? Are you serious?"

"John, listen, I've been trying to convince the people running KWIL that they should hire Janda back and pick up on the programs she was about to start. They're not going for it. We need to get going with Wand Enterprises anyway, I've decided—it's imperative. We've got a ton do. I need your help.

"Chris, I'm don't think I'm available. It looks like Judy's bank is going to hire me as an accountant trainee. I did some of that once too, you know, and I think I'm better suited for it. Doesn't it sound too good to be true? I've got a job! Chris, I owe it all to you."

This is the classic good news-bad news. I think my one-legged stool just broke "John, that's great, just great. Look, I…"

The door to the room opens and in comes Bob and Earnshaw and a blue-shirted security guy. Their faces look like somebody just died under a steamroller and they had to watch."

"Ah, the cops have arrived John. Get those reinforcements over right away!!" "Chris, what's happening?"

"Bye, John."

I hang up the phone.

"So, gentlemen, do we see it my way yet? I think my proposal is very reasonable and that Garder would agree if we gave him the opportunity."

Earnshaw is very stern now. "Mr. Walkman, I do not wish to be unpleasant, but we have concluded our discussion. Please leave my office."

"You didn't agree to my offer yet."

"Mr. Walkman, this gentleman will escort you to the ground floor and out of the building. Please be assured he is capable of doing it."

I size him up. Yes he is.

"I appreciate very much the time you devoted to considering these ideas, Mr. Earnshaw. I look forward to discussing them further someday soon. For now, I'm sorry but I must really rush off to my next appointment. Goodbye, Mr. Earnshaw."

I extend my hand for a shake. Our man in blue takes my elbow and starts walking toward the door with it. I shake him loose.

"Goodbye, Mr. Zemlin. It was a pleasure to see you today. I hope your ratings are everything you deserve!"

We walk out the office, toward the elevator. Earnshaw and Zemlin wave as the door closes on me and Mr. Blue.

Out into the lobby we go, and he sets me free like a wild trout that's just too small. Mr. Blue watches me swim through the doors onto the street. The air is full of street noise. I sink again into the eternal stream.

The reward I receive for my troubles is that my car is gone. I completely forgot it was in a no-parking zone. I haven't even got an idea where to go to find it. For some reason I don't even care. I'm not in the mood to screw with it. I just want to walk, walk and walk down Figueroa, down, down, down, feeling the swing of my legs, the swing of my arms, a nice rhythmic purpose of their own. My brain is filled with noise. Hello m'baby, hello m'honey, hello m'baby, hello m'honey." Record's got a scratch.

An hour, it takes me an hour, bumping into buildings, standing on fire hydrants, walking through hotel lobbies like some hopeful vagrant. I'm fully a man of the street, homeless and hopeless. After an hour I've walked over to the Blue Line station at Pico and Flower. It's only 15 stupid blocks south of City Hall. It was more bumble than bee-line.

But I welcome something new. You know, the Blue Line opened a year ago, and it's my first time here ever. We've got a new Disney ride right here in the city, and I've never been on it. One dollar and ten cents, coming right up. Stick it in the machine, here's the little ticket. Wait on the plastic seats. I wonder at the progress we've made. Maybe the automobile won't rule the day forever.

The horn finally blasts its deafening honk and off we glide down the street. Every city in the world has got something like this, what's the big deal with L.A. It's almost pure nostalgia having these cars here. We all miss the Red Cars.

South we head down the edge of North, then east on Washington, past The Bearing Man, machine shops, warehouses, graffiti everywhere. My fear is coming back as we head into, for me, darkest unknown territory, known a lot better to me actually since Saturday night.

Only 20 minutes later we slide into 103rd Street Station. Watts again. My beloved Towers rise from behind the trees one block away to the southeast. I can see them from the window. Off the platform, around the corner, stroll along the trackless railway bed, now the final resting place for a notice about the passing of Luther Washington, a fat man now gone but recently celebrated at the church I pass.

The Towers come closer, now hidden by a bungalow, now peeking between telephone poles. They rise and sparkle in the early afternoon sun. The sky is once again a gorgeous clear blue.

Here's a piece of blue ceramic tile on the ground. I pick it up. Sam, would you have used this one?

In the park, most of the trash from the festival has been picked up. I walk to the 10-foot fence that protects the shrine from vandals. The legend goes that the Towers are only damaged by tourists, never gang members. It's true, there's no graffiti on the eternal walls. And it's true that as the Watts Riots—or the Watts Revolution—burned businesses to the ground only blocks away, the Towers remained untouched.

I guess the message comes through. They are for, and about, the spirit of men. The gang kids may not live up to the challenge, to the role model, but I guess they know the idea is important.

I wave to John Outterbridge, the curator at the Art Center since 1976. He's the nice guy who said it was OK to bring our Window project down, too busy to talk right now at the end of the day. I'm not in the mood anyway.

What if everyone had the urge to build towers the way Sam Rodia did? They say that guy was really crazy. He drank and his wife walked out on him. He had only one single idea in his life: "I set out to do something big, and I did," he said.

What if everybody lived up to that? We'd be drowning in god damned towers I guess. Wouldn't life be boring, if anyone could do that?

Not everyone can, I guess. There was something in his toughness and orneriness and irascible nature. Irrascible—that's a word I like. Something about him said get the hell out of my way. Reminds me of Kenji, and Ivan, and Petra for that matter. That's something I really like about those people.

So what about all my cartoons? Do I just need to turn into an asshole and things can happen? The picture of me sitting in Earnshaw's chair comes back.

Whooo, wee! What an impact I had...the impact of me being back on the street. Maybe someone's got to be the follower, the dummy.

Looking up at the spires, just maybe I hear the sounds of a tiny little man, 90 pounds, a man with a hammer and trowel: tink tink, slice into the wet cement. Every single day for 30 years he climbed up the rungs with one bag for tile, the other for mortar. Put up some more color, cover and protect the steel.

Then one day it was done, and he left. Went up north to sit with his remaining family. Lived relaxed, like he'd done what he set out to do, and that was that.

As I walk around the back of a fence, here comes a gang, I know it's a gang god damn it. There's a bunch of tough kids. They've got blood in their eyes. I'm a dead man.

What do you say to a gang? Hey bro'. I'm chillin' out bro'. I don't wanna die bro'.

Why do they talk like that? These guys are wearing gang colors I know it. They must be the hoods of the 'hood, the neighborhood.

They clear the fence. Wait, I know—it's Abe Lincoln, the kid from Saturday night, and some friends!

"Hey, Abe. What's happening? It's me, Chris Walkman. Remember me from Saturday night? We had the Window thing out here."

The kid looks funny. He's on energy, or something. I don't deal with drugs much, but it looks to me he's on something. He can barely even look at me.

"Hiy Missr, hiy." Kids circle around. They are wearing colors, blue, they want to be with something, Crips or something.

"Are you guys a gang?" There's a feeling of fatal fascination in my question. "No, no!"

Sure, they're going to tell me. They're fogged over anyway. This makes me sad. The kid was alert the other day at least, with his mother.

"Where's your Mom, Abe? Is she around here anywhere?"

"Doan know. Mssr Walkman."

Maybe he's drunk. The other kids are the same way. They straggle by me, and head on out into the empty railway space. I'm dumbstruck. It's just something that happens every day, I guess, but it just makes me feel sad and pissed off to see human towers corrode.

THIRTEEN

By 6 o'clock, I've finally gotten my car back—$135 for towing and fines.

Nothing makes me more furious than parking tickets and getting my car towed. Life gangs up on you sometimes. The expense hurts, too. The $20,000 is all history, of course, and I've got about enough to last me a month. I saved one $100 bill for a keepsake of Ben Franklin. Maybe I'll frame it. He's even more of a hero to me now.

Whatever happens, I will never forget that happy rush the first time I saw his face.

Maybe John will help me account for the rest of the money in his new job.

My other problem is this disability thing. Seems like stuff is really piling up into big drifts around the fun house these days.

Its 6:30 when I get home and still light out on this summer day. The phone's ringing.

"Hello, Chris Walkman?"

"Robin Seesman here again, with the Institute of Psychological Difficulty and Clarification. I promised I would check in with you to see if you could use our help."

"Yes?"

"I notice here on a report I'm looking at that the State Disability Office is ready to look into your case more closely. I hope that is not too troubling to you, Chris."

"I've locked up all my knives, Robin."

"Perhaps I should come quickly to the point. I am associated with a gentleman I believe you know…Thomas Hugo?"

I almost drop the phone. "Yes, I know Mr. Hugo. What is your connection?"

"I will be candid with you. We are working with the state on a pilot program to see if we can help them reduce expenses on some of their programs, the Disability Insurance program being a key example. We believe that we can really help you out at the same time.

"Since it appears your benefits may soon be curtailed, I thought you might like to hear our offer. Could we chat with you this evening? Mr. Hugo and I can come see you right at your apartment. Thomas said he's quite anxious to meet you in person. What do you say?"

"What can I say? It sounds like you have an offer I should not refuse."

"Very well, Mr. Walkman. We'll see you quite shortly."

I have the feeling a little rat may be chewing on the inner-tube of my wheel of fortune. To get ready for their visit, I exercise, do some isometric worry.

Before you can say Jack Splat 400 times, there's a heart-stopping knock at the door and sure enough, it's that familiar star from the television screen, Thomas Hugo and his faithful sidekick, Robin. Fatman and Bobo.

"Good evening, Mr. Walkman." Not only is this scene playing like Hitchcock, Hugo even sounds like the guy.

We shake hands all 'round. Pump the handles, my uncle used to say. I invite them to sit on the couch. I sit in my cozy armchair which helps.

Efficient Mr. Robin says, "I'll get right to the point, Mr. Walkman. We at the Institute of Psychological Difficulty and Clarification, or at Thomas's company, Lifetime Adventures, which are in fact one and the same, are here to help you, and to help you help others.

"We have targeted certain carefully selected individuals for special investments and observation. Mr. Walkman, I must tell you that so far, you are one of our greatest successes."

"That makes me proud, I can assure you."

"The investment we made in you—"$20,000, I'm sure you've not forgotten it—was designed for just the sort of program you devised. We are so happy that our feeling for our subjects has been validated in such grand style. Aren't you, Mr. Hugo?"

"Yes, oh yes!"

He would definitely be a good Santa Claus at the asylum.

"The reason we have come here this evening is that, as I'm sure you can understand, we would like to work with you on a program that can support you, and will allow us a fair return on our already substantial investment. You understand this also helps the state by allowing them to cut back on disability benefits that you don't in fact quite deserve. It can protect you by preventing any legal action they might consider against you. Regardless of that, I'm sure that you would be so much more comfortable without the burden of guilt you face, isn't that so?"

"It's all true. You guys really do your homework."

That little rat has about chewed all the way through to the rim.

"Well, speaking of homework, let us explain our proposition. As you know, your recent associate, and ours, Mr. Kenji Komo, is no longer a credible candidate for our fund raising programs."

"Komo was your man?!"

"Yes he was, and a credit to the program as far as he went. He was doing so very well on the way back from his severe alienation after the strain of expectations his father placed on him. With hardly any guidance from us at all, he created the marvelous organization you saw, Knights of the Sun. Unfortunately, his verve and commitment ran away with the enterprise, and poof, his earnings base is no more—the donations I mean. I believe Mr. Hugo spoke to you earlier about the donations we like to see?"

"I recall that he did, yes, in what I presume are your offices on the 31st Floor of the Skyler Building?"

"Yes, though I believe you spoke through the TV communicator. That provides the extra bit of security we like. We were actually in the room next door which in fact is usually not locked."

That's not what I recall exactly.

"Anyway," Seesman continues, "as a result of Mr. Komo's misadventure with the mirrors we so generously equipped him with, and because of your poorly timed observations in the newspaper this morning, it's time for us to create another way for people to express their charitable feelings."

Hugo pipes up. "Chris, I know I was a bit blunt with you yesterday morning about the value of your show in Watts and Westwood. But, honestly I had not seen it. Robin here tells me you have created something quite special that deserves further support on our part. Are you interested in that idea this evening?"

I think I'm beginning to see a picture that is extremely interesting to me. A foundation for a very tall tower, as well as one of the most ambitious animated spectaculars ever undertaken, is ready for production.

Robin takes the ball again. "To be specific, we think the concept of Wand Enterprises as you outlined it is very appealing and would enable us, and you, to raise charitable donations in a very effective way. What we would like to propose to you tonight is that we plan a fund raising spectacular in the very near term that can really make a difference. I want to say right now that though our expenses and fees are not low, they are below 50 of the gross income, which is actually quite normal for this industry. And Chris, please make no mistake—this sort of thing is big, big business today. I hope you realize just how fortunate you are to have seasoned professionals on your side. The most important thing is that your excellent ideas will have a chance to get off the ground in a way you might never have dreamed. They'll have a chance to really do GOOD for people. Isn't that exactly what you've come to want in these two weeks since we met? Isn't that exactly the result of our investment in your own ideas? I believe you feel a stronger commitment than ever to what you believe. And that is what makes a successful program, isn't it?"

"Mr. Seesman, Mr. Hugo," I say, warming up now to an opportunity I had only been dreaming of, "you are exactly and precisely correct. I think we share a vision here that is quite stirring to me. I can't tell you how much I appreciate your support. I'd like to get started almost right away. What's the next step?"

They look at each other with very big smiles on their faces, and then look at me with renewed glee. I'm sure I look quite happy too.

Seesman says, "I think the very first thing we should do is sign this contract which outlines briefly the approach we've agreed on, specifically the 49 percent manager's fees and expenses due from the gross receipts of any charity received. But, please, let me assure you there will be plenty left over from which you can fund many, many good works.

"Then, we will draw up general papers establishing Wand Enterprises as a non-profit, charity organization based on what we understand of your plans and vision, plus some general bylaws that usually work.

"Then there's one final thing, and this is a very important point. Based on what we think will work very well with the public eye, we would like to offer you a facility that we think can serve perfectly as the center for Wand Enterprises. Does that sound like something that meshes with your thinking?"

"Very nice!" A lot of thinking is going on.

"Good. We have access to a former supermarket that has been closed for a long time. In a matter of days, we can arrange to have this store donated to Wand Enterprises by the former owner who will improve his tax profile in doing so.

"This store is in an area that you have indicated an interest in. Namely Willowbrook, just near Watts, a severely depressed area. We feel this will be sure to tug on heart strings with your audience, don't you think, Chris?"

"I think it's perfect." I really do.

"Our feeling in this matter is that one must always get the charitable operation up to some level of bootstrap success so that people won't feel they are starting it from nothing. They like their charities to be doing something already, is what I'm saying."

"Gotcha, I'm with you."

Hugo jumps in again. "What we would like you to do right away, Mr. Walkman, is to get with Janda Evers and, with her, speak to chairman Ned Garder of Modern Oil. They were pretty close, I believe. We think you have got to get him back on line with that TV station. Kenji Komo is lost to us. But we think you may be a fresh idea to Garder. He's a bit of an oddball, but basically sympathetic to charitable causes. I'm afraid we're not going to have a telethon at all if we don't get a station to do it, and with Mod-Comm's expansion plans, they are the people we want to work with. There are more than a few cities where this program can be of…assistance.

I just can't catch them licking their chops.

"Also, we are hoping the station will donate the air time. In our view this avoids some embarrassing difficulties with the IRS. There's so much less to investigate in the way of financial transactions, and so on. More money for all of us, eh?"

Boy these guys only want a few things.

I try to point out, "A lot of what you're talking about is impossible, or very unlikely, from what I understand of the situation at Mod-Comm. But, in general I like it, and I'll give it a shot."

"I do believe this all sounds reasonable," Seesman says. "To me, this is what you call a win-win-win situation! The Wand is our hook my boy, and it's a great one. Don't worry, we'll cover all the little details with the tax man, and you'll soon be doing very well. People drive Mercedes cars doing charity work."

Yes indeed, I couldn't have asked for much more of a custom-made way to move ahead with Wand Enterprises.

We exchange more pleasantries, and we sign this preliminary contract. I add the language I want in there, you know it by now. They are delighted with the principles.

Ideas are forming in my mind at an enormous rate. But one single idea is uppermost in my mind: I have GOT to see Janda.

As I close the door on my eager helpers, I call her up.

"Hello?"

"Hello, you don't know me very well, but I made you a promise earlier today about getting you back on a job. Can you spare a minute to talk about that? I think I may have some news."

Another stunning sales pitch on my part.

"Won't you let me come over, wherever you are? I'll just talk to you. I know you must be exhausted." Me, I'm lit up like a nuclear reactor about now.

She lets the question hang there.

"OK, Chris come on over."

Gulp.

Her apartment is in Los Feliz, upstairs, overlooking the Silver Lake. I walk up to the front door, ring the bell. Ancient ivy covers the flagstone exterior. I study this.

The door opens. There's a warm lamp behind her reflecting on the polished wood floor, a nice rug, couch, chair, woman in the door. Her brown hair is falling across her shoulder. She is feminine elegance itself, the warmest thing I have felt since years gone by. It's a bit of a contrast to my racecar heartbeat after my meeting with the sharks. She looks like a representative from another state of mind.

"Hello, Chris." Complete meltdown. "Hello, Janda. Thanks."

She stands there and it suddenly occurs to me she may not want to let me in.

"Can I come in?"

She stands there another second.

"Elvis told us, don't be cruel!"

"OK," she says. She steps back from the door as if she's on a hinge. She's pretty suspicious, and not very warm towards me still. She thinks she's got me, closes the door with a clunk and leans on the knob as if sometimes it opens up again after she shuts it.

"Can I offer you a…hot cocoa or something? How about a brandy?" She's bringing back Dollarz from the other night. It's a very friendly thing to do.

"Sounds really great." Her gentleness is easing me back a little.

We walk into a big living room with a gorgeous green herringbone carpet.

I've never seen anything like it. She's got some classic decanters on a tray. That's all it takes to suggest a fair amount of money. With grace, she pours a glass for me and a glass for her.

She turns. Hands me the glass. Offers a toast.

"I'm being nice to you, because I'm a Christian. I think idiots need to be endured."

That puts a new light on things, or cold water. I've suddenly got to ask where my head is. I'm on some sort of cloud after talking to those guys. Who is this woman? Why am I here? I need her. I want to push her somewhere, I forget exactly. She's just got my attention.

"What the hell is that supposed to mean, Janda?"

"It means that I think you did some pretty stupid things in your recent exploits. Here's to greater success for you in future, whatever different city you elect to try things out in."

"You mean this town's not big enough for the both of us, something like that?"

"Something like that, only different. I don't like people too close to me who knock me out of a very nice job and embarrass me in front of the chairman of our parent company. I think you'd agree I can thank you for that, Chris, isn't that fair?"

I put my glass down so it won't spill.

"Janda Evers, that is in fact a shitty bunch of stuff to say, because its god damned bullshit. You were pushing the edge over at your station, you even said so to me. I may take a PART of the blame for what happened today. But you said yourself you guys went TOO FAR! Own up to your own mistakes in selecting your friends, your idea people, will you?"

She doesn't say anything. I've got that slight trembling feeling. But I'm happy to get my feet back on the ground for a minute, too.

"I think that's especially unfair because I'm here to work on something else that I want to be good for you, OK?"

She does not look ready to back off. But I've got to try. There is a lot riding on this night all of a sudden.

"Look Janda, answer me one question, OK? Did you enjoy what you were doing with KWIL? Being creative, making things start to happen?"

She's still holding her glass like a human cucumber, looking at me, with little emotion.

"Yes, Chris, I did. You know it."

"Well, I think we should get back to that."

"Sounds fine. Let's hear the plan."

"There's a lot to tell. Wait a minute."

I look at her, then take my first drink of the brandy. I told John I don't drink much, and it's true. But this drink is a very necessary thing. The potent fumes rise straight into my nose, the liquid heats up my throat and goes into my chest. I can see those Saint Bernards looking good in the snowy Alps. Maybe I've been lost, too.

"You know, Janda, I think I'm kind of a fool, in many ways. I really think of myself as a lay-about, pretty much a good for nothing."

She's still unmoving and unmovable. I'm trying to get her attention. She's getting my confession instead. It's the power of a poker face.

"I probably owe California thousands of dollars in disability benefits that I didn't earn."

"So?"

"It's just starting to bug me, that's all. I'm not such a cynic or a bore."

"I know that. You're just a bit thick." I ignore the remark.

"Janda, I've decided I've got to do something. I think we both should start Wand Enterprises, together. What are you going to do otherwise?

"Regain my sanity. And find a job. Why don't you try that?"

"Look, I think when we get this Wand thing together, the way I see it, we can really get Garder signed up." I'm trying to get over to the issue.

I press on. "Garder will calm down soon enough. I think we can take your ideas, and the good people you've got, and mine, and Ivan and so on, and put something together. Then we'll bring Garder down, and you can help with that, and we'll sell him on supporting it. I think that's all pretty reasonable to hope, don't you?"

"How are you going to get the money to do this, to start up Wand? Got a place or something?"

OK, I've got to tell her.

"I do. I think we've got a chance to put together a facility that can look pretty good. With all the people we signed up over the weekend, we can do something pretty credible. And there's something else."

She looks at me with a slight air of question.

"I spoke to the people who were backing Kenji. Did you know about them?"

"Hugo, and Seesman? The fundraiser sharks?"

"Kenji was pretty evasive, but it was clear the money was not going to some cause. I never was really sure where it was going actually. What do these guys want?"

"They are ready to set up Wand Enterprises in a place, and set us up to do a telethon. They get 49 percent of the take."

She looks away. I don't think she's any happier about it than I am.

"Look, Janda, I know this sounds like a bunch of crap. But I think we can really do a fundraiser, and I think it can help get Wand on the way, right. I think the idea is so good, to try to do something good that really gets down into the problems, and really helps.

She still won't talk. But I'm coming to trust her as a sounding board.

"Janda, let me tell you a story. When I was small, my mother used to take me on her lap and tell me stories, just make them up. Sometimes we'd sit that way for an hour and she'd just make up things. She'd ask me what I wanted to have in the story, and I'd tell her, and she'd start to talk. I knew none of what she was saying was in her mind before she started, but within a few seconds she'd have us flying around the world, or rocketing way out in space among the stars. Maybe she'd dive us down into the ocean. Maybe strong wise people would visit our house and tell their own stories from out of the past. Always the stories were really wonderful. But even more than that was the idea that she just made them up, from nowhere. It was such a gift, but it's something that we all have got, the bringing of something to life from nowhere, just something inside our heads. I mean, to me, other than making a baby, there's nothing more special in the entire universe than coming up with something out of nothing."

She's still just looking at me.

"Janda, do you have any god damned idea what I'm talking about."

She finally nods a little nod. "Of course I do. That's what I'm all about."

I don't know why exactly but my eyes are filling up, brimming up, and suddenly I'm saying something I never say to anyone.

"My mom and my dad were killed one day by a man who wanted their money. He didn't have any, and he was very hungry. They never caught him, but mother told what happened before she died.

"That's sort of made me crazy for a long time. I don't know what it is meant to me. But it made me always look out for myself, and kind of screw myself over too.

"You know what the memory of her means to me?" I can't even see Janda for the ocean.

She touches my hand just very lightly, then sits back again and we both just sit there for a long time.

Finally I say, "Look, Janda, this may make you throw up, but I think I'm going to lay out some stuff so you and I can really see it. I've gotten to a point where nothing less than some kind of honesty will do. Are you ready?"

She nods. I'm completely in her power if she wants me. "So here goes, bitch!" We both smile and I'm done stalling.

"I think I am a guy whose image comes first. I am too worried about what people will think to really trust any ideas I've ever had.

"What am I up against? My own inertia and fear, that's what...a lot of 'can't do,' 'shouldn't do,' 'must do,' 'didn't do,' 'what would they think,' 'what do I think about that.' The monologue is deafening sometimes. Janda, you're so clean and directed. And Ivan and Petra, they're so clean and strong. And I walked around the Watts Towers this morning and looked at what Sam, or Simon, or whatever the hell is name is Rodia did down there. Why do these people make it seem so easy to have an idea and go for it, to trust a voice in there or something. Do you understand what I'm talking about? I end up almost inert, cannot MOVE."

She's just looking at me, her chin on her hand which is propped on her knee.

"Here's the part that drives me really crazy. I've got this idealism in me that says, hey this is America, of the Free, home of the Brave, I can be ANY...THING...I WANT TO BE. RIGHT?! Just dream it, then do it, off you go like RAMBO BLACK SAMBO, turn tigers to butter, just DO IT, shoot 'em up, or build a hospital, or raise myself by my bootstraps. We can all do miracles.

"Really most of me loves this part—sit around and dream up the impossible dreams, like...like Wand Industries. What a dream, to change the world. And this guy Hugo gives me $20,000 bucks because I DON'T KNOW WHY, and I run off like a drunken donkey kicking and jumping like a circus animal. And where does it get me. In a big mess.

"I don't know about you, but I think maybe I need a doctor or something, like you said over at DollarZ."

She smiles. "I was feeling fairly emotional at that point, Chris. I apologize."

"I thought you were right, don't you see? I mean how can I have such high expectations and such low confidence? It's a recipe for stalemate. Look at John. I swear the guy came to a full stop with his nose in the gutter because of just the same thing. Our whole country is based on this. You've got to tough it to the top somehow, or you're out.

"I just don't see where people can find the strength to fight it really, and not go crazy. Those gang kids, they've got it too, I think. Don't want to work. Life should be easier than that, they think. Yet everything about that decision to do nothing makes them just more of a failure. No money. Drugs make what life they've got seem great for a minute, keeps the myth going, but they get into a mess to support that. I don't know"

Again I sit.

"Chris, I think you're asking me for an opinion. I'm going to give you one unless you stop me. OK?"

"Shoot, said the condemned man."

"You know that your only real problem is not trusting yourself. It comes down to just knowing what you feel and what you believe, based on reasonable judgment, then sticking by that. It's very simple, really. Stand up for yourself as a man, Chris."

Her voice is like a million birthday candles.

"Janda, I guess there's no point in telling you that I love you, right."

"We can be great business partners, OK?"

"That's second best, by far."

"I'll tell YOU a story, though, which is outside of business a bit. Do you want to hear it?"

"Of course."

"I want you to know this thing about me, because it'll tell you what I want from a business partner, OK?"

"OK, Mom."

"Now you will make me barf, Chris. I am NOT your mom. I am a woman.

And I am a man. I don't say it out loud, it seems too stupid. But at least I will say it to myself.

"Tell me your story, Janda."

"When I was nine, I went to stay with my uncle in France. He spoke almost no English and I didn't speak any French. My parents thought I would learn by going there. I didn't learn any because I didn't stay very long.

"On about the fourth day, I went for a walk out of his cottage, thinking I would walk just a short way. But for some reason I kept going, and I walked all day, farther and farther from my uncle's cottage, until I had no idea where I was and really no idea how to get back. Finally, it was getting dark, but even at nine years old I wasn't scared. I realized that I did not care in the least if I ever got back. And it's not that I held anything against my uncle. I just wanted to wander and keep going."

She slumps into the memory, a happy place. Her eyes focus on a bit of fuzz on her sweater she's twirling gently in her long fingers.

"For me, Chris, I need no resting place in the world. Everything I see is something new to enjoy or experience with perhaps a new meaning, a new lesson. Knowing that, and loving that, is the essence of living, for me. I just want to keep finding things, new ideas.

"What finally happened to you, in France?"

"A policeman found me. He made me tell my uncle's name. And they took me back there. My uncle was furious and sent me home to L.A., back to my parents. They were not so angry, but they didn't understand either. To me it was such a simple thing. I wanted to wander and never stop, because the world never stops."

She looks at me.

"Chris, I do not want ever to stop in a single place with you. If we do something with Wand Enterprises, we must never stop looking for new things, new ideas, in our brains and in every person we meet. It is the way we will save ourselves, and everyone else."

"Janda, it broke my heart yesterday to see you withdraw from what you had started. Please come back. Please help us make Wand happen.

"OK, Chris. We're partners," she says, "but I tell you right now, I expect the best from you. I will never be your excuse or your cover for being less than your best. My trust means, give me the very best. We'll build a resource for the city, a model for the world."

"Yes," I say. I'm delirious at this real challenge.

"But there is still one major question for you. Can we get Garder to come on board for a telethon? Have we got a hope? I don't want to set him up either. Can you talk him into seeing us?"

"Chris, I can try. Let's talk tomorrow about it, OK?"

"Now can we go to bed?" she asks. My heart leaps. "By which I mean, me in mine and you go home, Chris."

Damn, life is never like the movies.

FOURTEEN

THE MORNING IS CLEAR, cool California summer as Janda and I head up the long Bel Air drive in Los Angeles to Garder's house. She got me the conversation I want and it's coming up. She's not doing the talking at all, she swears. I prayed her to, beseeched, wept and finally said forget it. I'm just going to treat this like a chat with dad, long gone, long gone.

Old Garder—which has a nice ring to it—has had a paternalistic feeling to him anyway, from the little I've seen and heard. He let his kids play till they went too far, then dished out stern results. Sounds to me he runs his Modern Oil Company like a toy train set, trying things out and letting the engineers scurry for position far below. I like that in a man.

It hardly occurred to me to seek him out downtown, certainly not to try very hard. Says something about my awe of power. It might have been a damn good idea.

Janda assures me that from her experience with Garder, I'd better be ready. "You don't get to be the lion at the top of a 33 million dollar corporate skeleton pile by being nice. You kill people." Instant death by being hurled over the bulwarks of his mountain-top estate is one possible outcome, Janda assures me.

At Janda's instruction, Coldwater Canyon produces a driveway on the left just south of Mulholland. We dive down the pine-lined drive, past the twin tennis courts, the helli-pad, the guest houses, and finally though a gate into an Italianate courtyard complete with imported cobblestones, Janda tells me. If I ever get a day someday, and an invitation, I might get to see the art collection. I'm not waiting for it.

We come to the front door, which is twice as tall as me. The door eventually reveals an imposing giant of a butler, from Frankenstein at Your Service, I presume. Frank leads us through the house and downstairs to the library where Ned Garder is reading and having his feet washed by a fussy little man.

Garder does not look up from his book. Nor does the washer. Janda motions me

It's a funny scene actually.

I review my intentions. Be natural. Be strong. Be clear. Be concise. Be friendly. Be courteous. Be brave.

We want to get him to donate the station time for a fund raiser on the Wand Enterprises building and programs. Robin and the Fatman are getting the building together. We'll have our stage, we'll have our reely big shoe. We just need a TV station to show it on. We're going to put out the word that the Wand Enterprises is open for business and there's an all-points bulletin for ideas that work, or could.

What if Garder says no? I'll ask him again. What if he says no again? I'll ask him again, politer. What if he throws me over the wall? I'll ask him louder.

"What's the toughest question he can ask me? That's a good exercise. Hm. Did you sleep with my Janda yet?"

That's a question and a statement. I look at the lady. She's got a wry smile.

She's used to this, I guess.

"Not for lack of desire, sir. But I believe the honor belongs to the bull." I'm not sure I'm heifer funny as I think.

"Son," he says, "the bull is just the one who does it. I leave it to your wisdom and Janda's discretion to take it from there."

Amazing.

"Janda tells me you want to bother me more about doing good and creative stuff. Why? Creativity don't dig up much oil y'know. Mostly sweat and skinned knuckles, an' so forth."

He holds up a left hand from which his middle finger is neatly missing.

"I hear a lot of high-falutin' bull in this city sometimes. Something tells me I may be in for a dose today, whether I want it or not."

"I have one question for you sir. How far does the FCC say you can go in using your station?"

"Not much farther or faster than I can pump oil or drive it according to the ICC. There's rules out there. I pay other people to worry about 'em."

Pretty matter of fact.

"Should I be worried about it, is that what you're sayin'?"

"Mr. Garder, to me it's like oil. You never quite know exactly what might be over the next hill."

"Got a point son." He looks at Janda, registering one for me, I guess. "So tell me something good over the next hill with my TV station. I see only trouble so far from you Janda." He turns to look at her, friendly enough.

I muse, "So far for your station I've seen only turkeys, with the exception of the lovely lady here. But what do I see for you...?"

Cranking up the brain cinema..."I have to believe you're a guy who likes innovation. Howard Hughes didn't do too badly with a new drill bit, did he? The whole history of the business is filled with discoveries and new ways of doing things. In fact, where were you till somebody could get the stuff out of the ground? I'd say invention is the cornerstone of the oil business. So that's one thing. Innovation could be good for your station.

"I know your main idea with KWIL is marketing, propaganda, and so forth. I mention the FCC because frankly sir, there only so many ways to promote your own products before somebody says your license ought to be reviewed. I can tell you from living here a while, going through a license review in this town is like having your bottom barnacles inspected in the town square. Everybody loves it, for years. I would bet that Modern Oil would solicit a number of comments on name recognition alone.

"So, my main question is what the hell you really think you can get out of the ownership? In fact, respectfully, I'd be curious to hear your answer. Why do you like the station?"

He's done with his foot bath and has gotten his fuzzy socks on and stuffed them down into some big cowboy boots. Saturday at home on the range. It's nice. I never quite expected Cowboy Biff, but so far, I'm really enjoying this.

Ned looks at me quite intensely. Any feeling I had that maybe I cornered him or got any skin is about to go away, something tells me.

"Son, listen up." His tone encourages that. I wait.

"Son…" He pauses again to lean back and tuck his shirt in better, while a soft little squeal of air escapes his lips.

"Son, I am a guy who got to where I am by being very, very sensible with my company. To me generally, that means not doing stupid things. The way I try to accomplish that is by listening to people who convince me they know what they're talking about. I know you met Mr. Earnshaw the other day. I could tell by your description of him you did, but he told me you did too. The man is a turkey, no two ways about it. But he is one smart turkey who has survived the chopping block a long time in the business he's in, which is communication between people in TV and like that. I have known him since we worked in Dallas together, and I trust that man.

"What I am trying to tell you here is this very simple thing. Bradford Earnshaw said that station would be a good idea for us now. It seemed like a good idea to me. It's not losing money. No station in Los Angeles is losing money. We bought the damn thing. We aren't losing any money, yet. I don't think any of that is very complicated, but I think it might answer your question. Would you like to ask Mr. Earnshaw any other questions about it?"

"What I would ask him is what it does for your business."

"Mr. Walkman, it brings us money by making money, and it brings us money by selling a little more oil."

It must be nice at night out there on the Prairie. I can almost hear the harmonica now.

I'm suddenly aware of Janda who's looking at me and registering points for the big man.

"Mr. Garder, let me cut to the quick here, if I may. I do not doubt for a second that your station is an outstanding move for you. Here are three of the simplest high falutin' ideas I can think of why you should support our telethon, and Wand Industries in the long run."

"One, there are an awful lot of people in this town who are not doing anything hardly at all except wasting time. I think we could put them to work for you almost instantly as idea men, sales men, foot men" (I'm looking at his boots and wishing I hadn't had the thought at all—I was thinking runners and so on) "and on and on.

"Every one of these people could be money makers if you planned to make it work that way.

"Two, in the long run, people are not going to be buying your oil, because they won't need it any more. Transportation is turning into communication pretty damn fast. Smog, and the Middle East and FAX machines are making this happen real quick. I know you are doing very well with the price of oil and all, but sooner or later, you're going to see diminishing returns. Cars get much more efficient. People go to work on TV and FAX, and so on. It would be nice to be in some other businesses about that time.

"Three, the very well intentioned and undeniably smart Mr. Earnshaw has not begun to deliver on the promise he made to make you more popular in this market with your station. Mr. Garder, with an investment equal to a small fraction of your regional marketing budget, you could become such a positive household name by doing good and generating trust you wouldn't know what to do with the customer loyalty.

"Let me conclude by saying that you can do all this by helping us address problems in the results-oriented way that you are totally familiar with in your day-to-day business, in the lowest cost way we can think of, using the cheap labor and brain power we have going to waste in this city, and by using the most highly leveraged and effective form of communication ever devised by man. By that I mean your television station and whatever others you might buy in the future." Janda flinches in her chair.

"What say you, sir, to this?"

Garder's head commences a little nod up and down, sort of a yes, more like a thinking. After a solemn minute of this, during which his eyes flicker in my direction, then Janda's, he says:

"My boy, this is what I will do. You get set for a telethon TV show in your Wand Enterprises place. And you get up and run that thing on one day. I give you one single chance to embarrass me so bad that I will feel no guilt at all in killing you with my bare hands. If you don't do that, son, you may have yourself a partner."

What's my heart doing around here by my two ears all of a sudden? It's like I'm deaf almost for the freight trains roaring by.

"Mr. Garder, I've got two more things to say. First, I need some start-up help on the place? Can you loan me $40,000 interest free for five years?"

"No; pay interest." He pauses. "Five percent." "No payments for one year?"

"Fine."

"OK. Two, I've got a hassle with the disability insurance office. I'm in the process of straightening it out, coming clean. I don't want you to be surprised about that. OK?

"Fine."

He's on to other things, stands up, scratches his hand in a circle down Janda's back and she leans at him just slightly. Speaks volumes. She's got a fabulously wonderful sexy smile on her face looking at me. She is all his.

Wand Enterprises is all ours!

FIFTEEN

"It's fine to be here with you today, ladies and gentlemen, on this really big day, for this really big show.

The location is our converted former supermarket at 120th Street in Willowbrook. The parking lot is planted with trees in pots, and bunting between poles. The mayor is here on the ample stage with me. The crowds are in a party mood. Word has gotten around in three months that something is coming down today!

I'm especially happy because Ivan is working one of the portable cameras.

We're just sad that Petra is not here. He has heard from her, but they are not together. She's off with Kenji right now.

Janda is here, a regal figure in red. And John never looked so good, I believe, as he does in his fine tuxedo. Many others whom you will meet are also here. Ned Garder is even here, in a finer mood than ever before, to hear Janda tell it. It's hard to remember what it was like the first day I surveyed the place with Robin and Hugo. It was depressing. Brown grass poked through all the cracks, broken bottles and paper trash, junked shopping carts lay tossed behind the chain-link fence. We didn't even have a key, had to slide under the gate, walk across the glass-covered asphalt to the front windows. Almost every square inch of exterior wall was spray-painted with graffiti.

Today it is still close to that, by careful design.

Our telethon show is well already underway, and with help from just about every kid in the neighborhood, the big sign is lifted to the top of our building. It just says WAND.

Everybody worked for weeks at the drafting tables to get just the right shape and size and color and style. All agreed it had to be primo graffito. It's in every spray-paint color from white to copper sparkle.

Three roving cameras, including Ivan's, are in and around and among the people. It's a controlled feeling of chaos and celebration, a lively party atmosphere for the viewers at home.

A cheer erupts as the sign settles into place and a lump forms in my throat. It is now hard to talk.

The sign completes the frieze of other graffiti on smaller pieces that circle the entire building. Each 2x2-foot board is a symbol of somebody who wanted their statement just there: Ducky and Zero and Neptune 9 and King Zad and there's no end to the signatures around the place. Around the entire fence out front too they stand five tall.

The main deal is that no spray painting is allowed on outside surfaces in the neighborhood except by express agreement of the property owners. In two months we've seen the incidence of unauthorized spraying decline by maybe 50 percent.

My biggest fear is that good kids will fight with rule breakers. So far, we've successfully insisted on peaceful means, and disapproval of fights in every channel has helped.

This is all an experiment, every little thing, day to day. But we've been in flower for two full months, no hassles, no fights, no bloodshed. I thank the Buddha and the great everybody else.

This entire place would not be working without the brilliant management and assistance of Jim Johnson who's great with kids and older folks. Way beyond his testing services, he's got natural abilities to find the most secret nugget of talent in anybody and turn it into gold. Eighty-five percent of it is his tone of voice saying, "Hey! I didn't know you were a mathematician! The way you saw in a glance that stack of boards was 20. Not bad! Now try this for a second," and he's off with a little exercise.

Jim brings great discipline as well to all the proceedings.

Can't say we're making money yet. I estimate a year. We're getting barter stuff like crazy, clothes and so on. An afternoon snack after school is covered every day, 100 kids in a rotation with 10 local restaurants who get dishes washed and vegetables brought down on the train in the a.m. from the produce market. Sanding cars is a big deal too, followed by paint jobs. We got it down to $30 and it's pretty good; guaranteed, too.

With all this activity we're creating a gravitational effect. The more we do, the more this is the place to come. That is a message itself: entrepreneurial thinking from a community perspective builds its own momentum.

The thing I like the best, which delivers on the name, is the drawing and drafting and designing room with a time clock and pencils and pens. Everybody who comes can clock in for some design time for dreaming and drawing. It works into a literacy and writing class for different levels. But I'm very big into making the connection between brain and paper, whether words or picture. Don't know where that's going to go, but we keep every intelligible scrap. We may get into a licensing operation before too long based on the name Wand and its designs. We'll create intellectual property of every description, from cartoon characters to artwork designs to names and styles and writing, a multitude of imaginings unimagined. It's a long-term thing for me. We may need an executive to make the sales and drive this business. And we'll determine a fair way to share royalties with the artists.

One of the many very tricky things about this place is private versus public property. For now, I've just decided it's going to be very complicated.

It's like this. By pulling together and pooling energy and talents against the economic odds, everybody helps everybody else. It's the first layer of our philosophy. But I'm a confirmed capitalist who says "watch out, or let the rip-offs begin." So we try to keep the contributions of each person as clear as possible with names and dates and so on.

This is going to get very wild if real money comes in for any reason. Dan Garder, are you listening? We could strike oil at any time! Then we're going to walk a tightrope between our rules,

"Respect their property, and yours" and "Help them if you can." Who's going to be contributing the most? That's the question.

To explain it, a sign is on the wall says, 'THIS IS A COMMIE JOINT RUN BY CAPITALISTS, OK?" We never really broke through the impasse that day at USC. How can something be mine and ours at once? "Calling all thinkers! Idea opportunity on the loose." I guess actually, Wand is a corporation with only contracted employees at the beginning. It's more than a school because it's out to earn money. How to share the wealth? Let's create that challenge first.

Also, we're trying to serve two different purposes. The Wand idea is meant to radiate and touch many communities, and ultimately stretch around the world. But each center is primarily a resource for its own community.

One of the most important things we try to do every minute is think of the person as an individual and touch his or her real wants and needs. That's fundamental in every organization like ours. We ask one important question of students or guests or workers: Are you going where you want to go and is that being as well defined as possible? Otherwise, all effort is wasted.

Tony Amboy is here a lot of the time, and people love him and his work with trash sculpture. He's not just doing found-object assemblages. He's trying to get real industrial artists and sorcerers involved, to create very usable and plentiful amounts of raw materials such as shredded plastic and broken glass. He's motivated by one main idea. If we show people useful, or elegant or expressive things made of reusable raw materials, they'll value the trash more. Its basic recycling. Glass, for instance, can be melted and fused into bars, wall decorations, and bricks. I think his strongest idea is that these things should be elegant and expressive in ways that grow attractively from the materials. He envisions museums of trash art. Not more trash art, you say!

Meantime, Tony's starting a band called The Wand that will help carry the creative anthem.

Carin Stoney has gotten together a small initial version of her locus hot-air balloon, in the shape of a chunky star with phrase "Wand Speak Up!" She's touring the city, becoming a gathering place to welcome new ideas and supporters. She's visiting campuses and shopping centers, inviting people to join with us to draw up solutions and educating on ways to break through barriers. Happily, today she's in the corner of the parking lot.

This is a miracle we've got here, no doubt about it. But it boils down to the vision of our team from Janda and the Window. It's also just the beginning. We're constantly reaching out and trying to build a relevant, exciting idea.

We're trying to be a central clearing house for all the good ideas out there plus data base, and referrals and advertising and, ultimately, funding if we can. Our biggest single challenge is to stay inspired by the idea that there can be solutions to problems.

I'm as hopeful as I have ever been that getting us out on the TV, Wand will spread the hope, inspire the thinking, and train the world's imagination to create on its natural, infinite scale.

Janda and I agreed we needed to pull Kenji back into Wand with a new agenda and bring Petra with him. They are reflecting on their navels by now! Also, we want to show Garder we could neutralize the danger and bring additional strength to our enterprise through his people.

Today, at our invitation, Kenji and Petra and Jeff Down are returning.

They've got army fatigues on, as if ready for battle. Behind them come mirror folks in a ceremonial walk down the street and into the yard. Their reflective attention shoots beams of light throughout our yard.

Slowly Kenji and Petra and Jeff ascend the stage. Janda and I hold our hands out to them and we touch.

I say, "Kenji, you and your people are welcome to the Wand. We recognize the value of your strength and commitment. You are a great leader. But the goals you espouse cannot be achieved through violence. Is this something you agree?"

"I do agree with this," Kenji says.

"In that case, Kenji, let's put on the very best show we know how."

Garder is on stage and thrilled by all the fun. The time has come for the questions.

"Ned Garter," I say on the stage, pressing a microphone close to him. "It's a pleasure to have you here representing Modern Oil."

"It's my pleasure to be here, Mr. Walkman. Congratulation to you on this big opening event."

"Thank you very much."

"Kenji, on citywide television, will you please ask Ned Garder, the chairman of Modern Oil, the owner and operator of this TV station, the question you would like to ask about his company's future energy plans?"

"Chris, it would be a pleasure." He turns to Ned.

"Mr. Garder, please tell us what your company plans to do about reducing our nation's dependence on fossil fuels and thereby reducing the spread of the greenhouse effect in coming years?"

"Kenji, it's a pleasure to speak to you today and I'm happy to answer that question. We intend to continue our research and development of solar power, wind power and other alternative fuel sources. We fully support reasonable fuel emission standards. We continue to develop fuels that will not be dangerous in use.

'We encourage the development of public transportation and far more efficient vehicles.

"I'm also happy to say we are more interested than ever in the form of communication you see going on right now. I believe strongly that television and other electronic media are the appropriate transportation mode of the future. As a result of recent events, and partly motivated I would admit by your own courageous leadership, we have now decided to substantially increase our commitment to telecommunications. That, in addition to the other pollution control programs I mentioned, will I hope lead to a better world for us all.

"We do not intend to abandon our current business. But as even our most critical shareholder can agree, these new endeavors are important to us all."

I chip in. "Kenji, as you are poised there again with a symbolic grouping of your mirror team ready to melt our resistance, do you have any reactions to this?"

"Chris, and Mr. Garder, I am proud that we have come to agreement. We will not cause damage. I look forward to supporting the company in its new endeavors."

I'm glad to see that force has yielded to a winning negotiation. I think Ben Franklin would have been proud of me.

"Thank you, Kenji." Garder speaks again.

"Chris, if you will permit me to continue for a moment. We make another commitment today, to developing energy of a very different sort. I'm talking now about the most precious resource of all—the people of this nation and the world. We must, and we WILL do everything we can to support individual dignity, self-esteem and productivity.

"I believe that Wand Enterprises, with its quest for innovative and effective solutions, along with the many, many good ideas and programs already in the works, in government and elsewhere in private industry, will soon cause a retreat in the timeless tragedies of poverty, illiteracy and despair. We are committed to the search for solutions with the belief that a real solution may be only one good idea away.

"Solutions do exist!"

He bows and goes.

"Thank you again, Mr. Garder," I say. "It was truly an honor to share this stage with you. And thank you again Kenji."

"You know, ladies and gentlemen, today we are beginning something fairly new in the world of telecommunications. Normally it looks, with this sort of program, that we are ready to ask for your money.

"This program is a little different. This place you've been touring today, courtesy of our outstanding camera crew, stands for the power of good ideas. Today, I'm going to express my confidence in the excellence of those good ideas by saying we don't need your money.

"Today, if anything, we seek your investment. And even at that, send no money please.

"The investment I ask you to make today is one of faith in the spirit of man's mind to dream, to refresh us with the cool water of inspiration when the landscape of the old is parched.

"So relax in the knowledge that kind benefactors have already laid the groundwork for our success. All I ask you to do, is watch us grow in the coming months and years. And bring us ideas when you have them. Bring us your challenges too. We are here, a deep cool well of confidence that solutions do exist. And when there is a well, there is a way. It is as simple as that.

"As a final expression of this confidence I intend to honor with you now an outstanding group of people whom you have not met before. They normally like to operate behind the scenes."

I can see that Ivan is rising up in the elevator now.

"As you see on the screen here, our outpost camera is ascending into a building downtown. We're going to visit two people whom I know you will enjoy meeting."

Ivan is doing a great job and has found the office we want. He's heading through the door which is not locked today. I believe he made sure of that.

"Ladies and gentlemen, it now gives me great pleasure to introduce the two people who have made this facility possible. Mr. Thomas Hugo and Mr. Robin Seesman who found this building and leant the funds to make it ready."

Ivan perfectly times his move into the room. These gentleman do not look happy. They are flustered like Laurel and Hardy.

"Mr. Hugo, I believe you can see me on your set. Am I right?" Our editor cuts back and forth between them and me. They are paralyzed on the couch, mouths hanging open.

"Uh, yes, Hi Chris. It's a pleasure to see you. Thank you for the honor of recognizing us in this way."

"The pleasure is all mine. Ladies and gentlemen, in gratitude to the investment that these men have made in The Wand. I am pleased to award them today a check for $40,000 to return them to the solvency they deserve.

"And gentlemen, if you would be so kind, let us destroy the contract that is now of no use to you. There will be no donations to Wand Industries.

Hugo jumps up and grabs the papers on the desk where they lay.

"This contract is one they normally employ when they assist charities that do accept donations. Since this version is not relevant to us, they have agreed to tear it up right in front for all to see, isn't that right, Mr. Hugo?"

He can hardly refuse. He does what he's told. Garder's $40,000 sapped any resistance he might have had.

It is a wonderful moment for everyone concerned, and a terrific way to launch Wand Enterprises.

"Now, as we begin what I hope will be a new chapter in health and peace for the world, let us revel in the sound of Tony Amboy and the Wand Band!

And they begin a rousing musical tribute to those who believe in cartoons—that they may one day come true.